Jane's bearings shifted. Her uncomfortable awareness of being seated with a group of women watching another woman dance faded and she was aware only of Ramona's lithe body dancing for her.

And she knew it was for her.

Her stomach quivered. Her nipples drew lightly with pleasure. Warmed by the whiskey, she lost herself in Ramona's flashing eyes. She envied the dance of the moonlight on Ramona's long slender neck. Her fingers ached to follow the shimmering line of her shoulders. Jane's eyes hungrily took in the grace of Ramona's fingers as she raised her arms in supplication — beckoning the moon above Jane's shoulder to come dance with her. To be her lover. Jane's body responded hotly to Ramona's enchantment and overrode the feeble warnings her mind sent to try to break the spell.

The women shouted, stamped their feet and clapped their hands to the heated rhythm. All except Jane — who sat immobile, mesmerized by Ramona's beauty — by her open invitation — her promise of . . . of . . .

Sex. Ohmygod! What am I doing? I can't do this! Jane crossed her arms over her midsection and felt her heart thumping wildly beneath her ribcage.

The music stopped. Ramona flashed a smile round the circle, curtsied and wrapped herself in the blanket Lu held out to her. She sat across from Jane and looked at her from smoldering eyes that hid nothing. Nothing at all.

Special Thanks:

To Barbara Grier of Naiad Press — who, with her unswerving vision, dedication and commitment has given 'the lesbian in literature' a larger, friendlier world.

To Katherine Forrest — whose landmark novel, *Curious Wine* is a beacon for us all.

To Ann Klauda, my editor, whose discerning eye and invaluable suggestions are helping me to become a better writer. (Thanks, Coach.)

To the members of my writing group whose critique and support are as necessary as air.

And to Susan, my heterosexual-married-feminist-friend, who read this story when it was young and pronounced it "not either silly" and said I should finish it and publish it. Here it is, Susan. Thank you.

WILDERNESS TREK

DOROTHY TELL

The Naiad Press, Inc.
1990

Printed in the United States of America
First Edition

Edited by Ann Klauda
Cover design by Pat Tong and Bonnie Liss
    (Phoenix Graphics)
Typeset by Sandi Stancil

Library of Congress Cataloging-in-Publication Data

Tell, Dorothy, 1939—
    Wilderness trek / by Dorothy Tell.
        p.   cm.
    ISBN 0-941483-60-6
    I. Title.
PS3570.E518W55   1990
813'.54--dc20   89-48972
                                                     CIP

For Ruth — light of my life —
lover, partner, friend —
forever.

About the Author

Dorothy Tell is the pseudonym of a lesbian grandmother who lives and writes in Texas with her lover of seventeen years. She is an apprentice crone who will always believe in the Christmas Fairy. *Wilderness Trek* is her first novel in the Poppy Dillworth series. *Murder at Red Rook Ranch* (coming soon) is the second.

Table of Contents

1

Needs and Expectations

A sleek, one-eared calico cat curled around a pot of cactus on the windowsill. She eyed the two inhabitants of the room regally. Her missing ear and a patch of dark color across one eye gave her the panache of a pirate queen.

A very tall, dark-haired woman toyed with the handle of a blue cup. She absently sipped the contents, and with one hand repinned wisps of hair into a bun at the nape of her long neck while trying to listen to what her visitor was saying:

"How long has it been now, Ramona? Harold is gone. It's time for you to get on with your life. It's not good to grieve forever."

Ramona's carefully chic visitor waved a smooth hand as if to sweep away Ramona's objections. "I know you loved him, but, darling, two years is an exceptionally long time to closet yourself. The chamber group suffers the lack of your accomplished hands at the piano. We all miss you. Besides, there are men out there in the world. What about your needs, dear?"

Ramona placed her cup carefully in the saucer and lifted her chin impatiently. Large brown eyes and high cheekbones revealed her Indian heritage. "I don't even know if I *have* needs, Delores. Anyway, I appreciate your concern and I *am* making plans to get myself 'back into the world' as you put it. A young woman who works at the art gallery suggested something to me that kept coming back to mind until I acted on it."

The cat claimed Ramona's attention by suddenly looking at her with something close to interest. Delores extended her hand toward the cat but drew it back as Ramona said, "Don't waste your time. Scrapper's never been anyone's cat but Harold's."

Proving a point, Scrapper stretched, rose, moved just out of reach and lay down again, making optimum use of the warmth of the sunlight. She crossed her front paws and turned away from the women to pay closer attention to a large garden spider outside the window that was busily spinning a web between two graceful urns.

2

Delores prompted, "Well, dear. What is it? What're you going to do?"

Ramona looked away from Scrapper and down at her empty hands.

"I've signed up to go on a wilderness trek. I need to get out of San Antonio for a while. I expect to get some photographs for a new series of watercolors."

"A trek! Darling, how exciting. Where? Africa, Canada, the Amazon? Who is the guide? Is he anyone we've heard of?"

"Um . . . well, actually it's a two-week trek in the Ozark mountains of Missouri and it's for women only."

"The *Ozarks*! You could come with us to Antibes. Or with Sasha and James to Majorca. Gawd! The *mountains*? With *women*? Ramona, have you lost your mind?"

"No. At least I don't think so . . ." Ramona's low voice trailed off as she speculatively returned the gaze of the old cat on the windowsill.

* * * * *

Three hundred miles away in Forth Worth, Texas, Jane Jackson backed her blue Toyota truck out of her son's driveway. From the tape player soothing waves of a Mozart concerto rose and pulsed around her. The music filled her chest and torso with a release similar to sexual orgasm. Chillbumps formed on her long arms and legs as the air conditioner breathed foggily into the little cab.

She became sharply aware of another sound and turned her eyes back toward the house where she had just spent four days babysitting her year-old

3

grandson. Her daughter-in-law, Rina, ran toward the street, waving and shouting. Behind her, at a trot, came Jane's son, Wolfe. He carried a screaming child out away from his body like a pinioned monkey. Tiny hands and feet clawed at the air, seeking purchase anywhere.

Jane set the brake and was out of the truck at a run to see what calamity could possibly have happened in the few seconds since she said her goodbyes on the porch. She didn't see any blood. Sky wasn't behaving like a *hurt* baby anyway. More like an *angry* baby having a fit.

"Mama Sis! Where did you put Sky's passies?" Rina, red-faced from the dash to the street, looked sheepish as Jane placed her hand over her breast and sagged a little when she realized no one was hurt.

"Oh." Jane raised her hands to her temples and kneaded the place on each side where the ever-present, nagging pain had increased to a pulsing thud. She mentally searched for the mega-important pacifiers. "I sterilized all of them. They're in a jar in the cabinet above the dish drainer."

Upon hearing this, Wolfgang waved, turned and made quickly for the house, still carrying the unhappy child at arms' length. Rina stood on tiptoe and hugged Jane for perhaps the tenth time in the past hour.

"Thanks again, Mama Sis. We had a wonderful time at South Padre. You were right. We did need some time by ourselves. Thanks for making it possible. Now you go on and get ready for your vacation trip up to the mountains. When you come back through Denver be sure to give our love to Isadora."

She kissed Jane on the cheek, then followed Wolfie back toward the house and away from the already searing heat of the sun.

Jane half-turned toward the street, then remembered she hadn't given them her trip itinerary.

"Rina — wait up!" She dug in her pocket and produced a neatly folded sheet of paper. She smoothed it out on her knee and handed it to her harried daughter-in-law. "That's a map of where I'll be and a list of phone numbers, but if you need me, you'll have to get the Missouri state police to find me once we get up in the mountains. For two whole weeks I'll be out of reach."

Rina took the paper and tilted her head. Her eyes twinkled with something Jane couldn't quite identify. "Thanks, Mama Sis. I think we'll be okay. But, I wonder if maybe you aren't more worried about *you* not being able to get in touch with *us* than the other way around?"

"I . . . oh . . . well," Jane laughed nervously. "Well, anyway, I feel better if I know you all can reach me. Of course, I sent one of these to Mother and to your Aunt Portia and Aunt Carol Lou."

One more sweaty hug and Jane was on her way. She had cut the time close. There were still things to be done at home in north Dallas, which was still an hour's drive away. Tomorrow morning she would be on the highway to the first real adventure she'd had since her college days twenty-five years ago. A wilderness trek. Maybe she could recapture some of

5

the enthusiasm of her childhood. Rekindle a zest for life.

God, am I ready for some peace and quiet and time to think. Jane rubbed vigorously at a tight muscle in her shoulder and thought about the serenity of nights in a sleeping bag under the stars.

2

Life in the Fast Lane

Lu held the Jeep speed at an even seventy with an eye out for the Highway Patrol. The tires whined in protest against the hot pavement of the interstate. Seventy was faster than Lu wanted to travel, but Desiree, her lover of twelve years, sat on the edge of the seat like a Russian wolfhound poised for the signal for the hunt to begin, her perfect nose pointed into the wind and her long blonde hair streaming away from her sleek head and neck, while the polished nails of both hands drummed a clicking tattoo on the dash.

Desiree turned the full charm of her green eyes on Lu. "How far is it *now* to Dallas, hon? I mean, in minutes?"

Lu grinned. "You sound like Beaver Cleaver. Don't get your panties in a wad, sugar. We'll be there soon."

Desiree furrowed her forehead, bringing her carefully tweezed eyebrows together in an enchanting frown. She curled back her lip and hissed displeasure at Lu. "Let's stop at this next rest area. I need to pee. My legs are stiff and my arm is getting sunburned. I wish this thing was a convertible. Then we could put the top down — it's such a beautiful day."

Lu glanced sideways. "Okay. We'll stop, but it's a good thing we *can't* put the top down. You'd just get your whole body sunburned then. And that reminds me, Des. Just before we left, Kay told me there'll be three straight women on the trek this time. So you can't run nude through the woods and put on a show like you did last year."

Desiree glowered, crossed her slim arms across her midsection and sat back in the seat. She shot questions at Lu. "Who? What kind of straight women? Where are they from?"

"A new grandmother from Dallas, a Junior Leaguer from San Antonio and a missionary from Austin."

Desiree leaned forward, resting her chin atop her laced fingers. "You're right. My life is over."

Lu slowed the red Cherokee at the rest station off-ramp. Lu locked the Jeep and went to check out the restroom with Desiree. Satisfied the sweltering room harbored no maniacs, Lu walked slowly up and down the sidewalk keeping to what shade the stunted trees provided, making sure her view of the vehicle and the restroom entrance was unobstructed.

Desiree soon emerged from the shadows of the restroom gateway, turned toward Lu and assumed a classic hitchhiker pose. She had removed her T-shirt and was now clad only in a brief halter top and shorts, the cuffs rolled high up on her thighs. Lu caught her breath at the sight of Desiree's long shapely legs. She was still the most beautiful woman Lu'd ever known.

Lu was so mesmerized by the sight of her lover sauntering toward her that Desiree's arms were around her neck before she noticed the flashy chrome-studded semi that ground to a smokey stop behind their Jeep. The driver expressed emphatic approval on his air horn as Lu frantically pried Desiree away from her side.

"Come on, idjut, before Bubba there invites himself along!"

Desiree strolled to the Jeep, rolling her hips in exaggerated burlesque, greatly amused at the shrieking of the horn and the truck driver's "Hey heys!"

Lu efficiently unlocked the door and pushed the giggling Desiree inside. They shot onto the ramp with a scatter of gravel and swirl of McGarbage.

Lu tried to retain a degree of dudgeon but

Desiree's laughter was hard to resist. She loosened her grip on the wheel and looked at her lover intending to admonish her, but simply melted instead.

Desiree was busily slipping her shorts and panties down past her knees.

Lu sucked in deep lungfuls of fresh air from the open windows, trying to keep enough attention on the road to hold the vehicle on course. Desiree had shucked her silly mood along with half of her clothes and was now, Lu knew from long experience, seriously intent on orgasmic relief from the boredom of the trip. Thank the Goddess for divided highways and wide open spaces. Any on-coming traffic would pass too far away to afford the drivers even a glimpse of lesbian passion.

Desiree scooted over as close as she could to Lu, took Lu's right hand from the wheel and laid it gently on her bare upper thigh. Lu brushed her hand lightly over Desiree's legs and thrilled to the familiar feel of her lover's warm, damp pubic fuzz while she kept at least one eye on the rearview mirror. This was no time to give a truck driver reason to run up their tailpipe.

Desiree spread her legs and pushed her hips forward. Lu dipped her first two fingers into the cleft there. Desiree grasped Lu's hand and held it to her as she thrust her hips up and back to the tempo of the drum music from the tape player.

Lu had never ceased to be surprised and pleased by the mercurial woman who now moaned in orgasm, uninhibited on the seat beside her. The exquisite excitement of driving down the interstate with her fingers buried in the pulsing vagina of a beautiful woman weakened Lu's knees as Desiree rapidly

10

achieved her second orgasm. The "bitsy" one, she called it.

"Holy Hera, Des, hurry up," she teased. "I think my hand's going to sleep."

"You don't want me to hurry up, you liar. You want to sit on my face." Desiree curled against Lu like a cat and nipped at her earlobe.

"Well, you're right about that, sugar, but I'm going to take a raincheck on my turn. I want to get to Poppy's in one piece and I don't think I could actually drive and do it at the same time. Besides, I think that's Bubba from the rest stop coming up fast in the passing lane."

Desiree laughed a series of satisfied little ha-has and hastily dressed as Lu squirmed against the temptation of letting Desiree investigate just how much of the wetness between Lu's legs was perspiration. Her foot lowered on the gas pedal and the red Cherokee pulled decisively away from Bubba and his straining Peterbilt.

* * * * *

Desiree, calmed by the pulsing release that still claimed her vagina, looked over at Lu with a great rush of love and gratitude. What an Amazon. What a *woman*! She took in the sight of Lu's crown of thick, coppery-red hair, the way the sun glinted through the wavy length of it.

"Thank you, darling. I love you," she said simply to her lover's profile.

"You're so very welcome, m'dear. Me too, you."

"This camping trip's going to be fun. Away from that damned hospital. I don't want to think about

11

anything but us for two whole weeks up in that valley. It's the same place we went with Poppy and Irma that time, isn't it?"

"Yeah," Lu answered pensively. "You know, hon — it's been four years since Irma died. Doesn't seem possible, does it?"

"Nope, sure doesn't," Desiree answered. She thought it also didn't seem possible she'd just passed her thirty-second birthday. Where had all the time gone? Being a nurse had lost a lot of excitement she had felt years ago. Disenchanted was the word that came to mind. Well, maybe during these two weeks she could gestate and birth an idea that had taken root in the back of her mind. Maybe she could make Lu understand — make her see the necessity of a major life change and what it could mean to the two of them.

Lu was always so *practical* though. But, if she worked it just right, Desiree thought, Lu would come around.

3

Tickets and Destinations

Poppy Dillworth moved slowly through each room of her home at fifty-five-twenty Mistletoe Street. She buffed the brass gascocks to a shine with a worn bandana as she turned each one off at the wall.

Twenty-two years of loving attention had made the old buff brick into an "M-Street" showplace. Gardens surrounded the many-chimneyed house with its spectacular, colorful leaded-glass windows, each opening graced by a delicately designed flower. Soft inside lights at night lent the house the appearance of a sanctuary. During the day the Texas sun streamed through the windows in bands of multicolored light, bathing the interior in a happy glow.

Poppy removed her glasses and absently cleaned them on her shirt cuff. She ran a hand through close cropped, curly white hair and replaced the spectacles. She lowered her aging yet still graceful body into a padded rocker placed where she could concentrate on her favorite window: the one Irma had designed and made for Poppy's sixtieth birthday, just a year before cancer took Irma away from Poppy forever. One single warrior iris commanded the center of the window, waving its purple blooms above graceful blade-like leaves. Stylized clouds rose up in the distance where a rainbow arched between them.

A pool of purple and green light from the window fell on a worn braided rug at her feet, the rug where Ellie used to curl up and dream canine dreams. The day Poppy had brought the gangly springer spaniel home, Irma had taken one look at the pup and exclaimed, "Oh Poppy, she's such a homely little thing. She looks just like Eleanor Roosevelt."

Poppy rocked slowly. Irma gone. Now Ellie, too. No one left with whom to spend her longed for, toiled for, *dearly* paid for retirement. She longed for the peace of the mountains. Her bruised and aching spirit sought relief from what her life had become.

A soft pealing of door chimes and calling voices broke upon her solitude. *Humph — if the damn dog hadn't died, I'd'a known they were here before they got on the porch. Damn quiet. Damn quiet empty house!*

"Yoohoo! Pops . . . you in there?" The top of Desiree's head appeared, disappeared, then appeared again as she tried to jump high enough to see inside through the tiny rose window beside the doorway.

Poppy yanked the door open. "Of *course* I'm in here. Half the neighborhood's dead, but *I'm* still here."

Poppy hugged the two women. Every year they seemed to get taller. *That raucous blonde's got legs all the way up to her armpits. That redhead — look at that stuff wave. Bet it's long enough to sit on.*

Poppy's inner dialogue was repeating itself these days. Boring development. Judgmental old busybody. Hardly better than no company at all.

"All this stuff ready to go?" Lu waved a hand toward the pile of camping gear beside the door.

"You bet."

Lu grabbed the backpack as Desiree gracefully swung the bedroll to her shoulder. Poppy's new walking stick clattered to the floor. She bent to rescue it, but Desiree beat her to it.

"What's this? A shillelagh? Whatcha gonna do with this thing, Pops? Beat off marauding chipmunks?"

"I'm gonna *walk* with it unless you *talk* it to death."

"Hey." Desiree's face suddenly sobered. "Where's Ellie?"

"Aw, she finally gave up her doggy little ghost

15

last fall. I buried her in the back yard out by the herb plot." Poppy cleared her throat to relieve the anguish that began to constrict it.

"Oh, Poppy, I'm so sorry." Desiree dropped the bedroll and a stricken look replaced her usually arch expression. "Can I go see?"

Poppy caught Lu's warning look that was meant for Desiree, but Desiree had already headed for the back door.

Oh well. What the hey. No matter any more. Maybe Old Dog's spirit's still hanging around somewhere. Might be happy to see all that blonde hair and bare legs. Woulda had a crotch-sniffing frenzy if she was still alive.

Poppy watched from the kitchen window as Desiree knelt by the little monument beside the fallow herb garden. The usually neat borders of the flower gardens merged with the edges of the weedy herb plot. No reason to plant this year.

Poppy didn't go out. She'd already said her goodbyes. She only half heard the musical sound of the two women's voices as Lu comforted Desiree. The news of the dog's passing seemed to have unlocked an uncharacteristic flood of emotion in Desiree. Poppy watched impatiently as Lu held Desiree close and stroked her hair.

Well, tough noogies, girls. That's the way it is Out Here In The West. You buys your ticket and you takes your ride.

"Thank you, Wondercrone." Poppy spoke sarcastically to her inner voice. "I couldn't've made the morning without that little nugget."

* * * * *

16

Some many miles to the north a plump young woman was nearing the end of her own ticketed journey. She riffled the pages of a small New Testament with her thumb. Her eyes came to rest on the inside of the front cover where she read:

Given to:
Marcie Hazel Judy, Missionary in Training
God be with you when you are
called for your first mission.
Yours in Christ,
Dr. Garland Belcher, D.D.

She glanced around at the other passengers on the Greyhound bus. Large black women with many small children. Young white men in ill-fitting clothes with expressions to match. A couple of surly bikers dressed in chrome-studded black leather. Frail old people of all colors and descriptions. A fertile ground for a fledgling missionary. She tried to find just one set of eyes in the sea of faces around her that seemed in the least receptive. She caught her own reflection in the window.

Oh wow. That's great. I don't even look like I would listen to myself.

Marcie surreptitiously hitched up her bra, then closed the little Bible, veteran of many sword drills. She pushed it into her backpack where it found a place amid an assortment of candy bars and cookies. The Missouri landscape flowed past her tired eyes. She thought about her destination. A two-week trek into the mountains.

Not enough self-reliance. The words still burned her inner ear. Well, surely this would show Miss Paul

17

that Marcie was tough enough for the post in South America. The committee would be surprised when she came in for her application session. She fantasized about their surprised, pleased response to her show of independence.

Finally after all the years of floating aimlessly from one dull job to another, from one disastrous love affair to another, she had finally, almost earned a title. A label. Soon she would belong somewhere. Thirty was a little late in life to start out, but she would make up the time. She knew her mind was not quite in the right place. Never seemed to have reached that sublime plateau or achieved that peace that "passeth understanding," but her *heart* was okay. Her *want-to* was torqued to a high degree of tension.

It must have been God's will that delivered the flyer advertising the trek into Marcie's hand. Though it did puzzle her that the intense young woman who gave it to her at the bookstore seemed to know she needed "something like this." Mysterious ways, indeed.

She felt just like Maria in the *Sound of Music* when Maria left the convent. But, no — not *exactly* like Maria because Maria ended up in a whole lot of —

The bus slowed to a hissing stop. The driver craned her long neck around when no one rose to get off.

"Hey, lady!" She jabbed a bony finger at Marcie. "You asked me to stop here. You gonna get off or what?"

Marcie grabbed her backpack and lurched,

blushing, up the aisle, trying to get a look at the RV park through the windows.

"Thanks," she mumbled, forgetting the godblessyou, and barely made it off the step before the bus moved off in a black cloud of diesel smoke. She coughed, eased her bra strap back up on her shoulder and turned to find a muscular blonde woman extending a hand toward her.

"Howdy pardner, I'm Kay," she boomed. "You Marcie?"

4

Pocahontas Meets Jungle Jane

A part of Ramona's consciousness noted that a small blue truck had stopped beside the two Jeeps, but her attention was centered on the sky above the western horizon. Bands of hazy purple layered upward into clear blue. She swept the distance with her gaze, mentally cataloguing the changing shapes and hues of the rolling foothills. She turned away finally from the breathtaking panorama and found herself looking directly into eyes the same color as the sky.

She tried to break contact with the unclouded blue eyes and fought to recover her customary poise. A tremor buzzed between her shoulder blades, a physical stirring that quickly translated into a blush.

Rarely was a woman tall enough to look straight into Ramona's eyes. In fact, at an even six feet, Ramona was taller than most men. She smiled a brief acknowledgement to the handsome woman in front of her and began to turn away.

"What were you looking at way up there?" asked Sky-eyes, who kept her hands in her hip pockets and gestured with her chin at the portion of sky Ramona had been studying.

"I was memorizing the colors so I can paint them when I get back home."

Through the years Ramona had developed a habit of focusing on a distant point above people's heads, a habit which allowed her to maintain some emotional distance. Just now she was having trouble breaking away from the intensity of the blue eyes locked with hers.

All natural flight begins with a tiny movement deep in the center of some pulsing ovum or dark cocoon — and Ramona desired flight. She wanted to be somewhere else. Anywhere else. The jagged edge of feeling between her shoulder blades spread into a warm unsettling awareness in every cell in her body — the sudden celebration of every hair moving in the slight breeze. She turned away, struggling to regain composure.

"I must write down the colors while I still remember them," she said over her shoulder as she hurried toward her backpack for her notebook. She noted as she left that Sky-eyes' nametag said *Jane*

Jackson. And that Jane Jackson stood frozen into one posture. Her elbows stuck out in back, each hand jammed palm to butt in the back pockets of her green safari shorts. Her open, friendly face seemed to register puzzled regret as Ramona walked away.

Ramona knew she had acted strangely. She was unnerved by the reaction of her body to the direct, piercing gaze of the woman who had spoken to her.

Ramona moved quickly to transmute this energy to the pages of her sketchbook. She annotated the just-completed sketch and sensed someone standing close behind her. She turned as the tall woman reached out to tap her on the shoulder.

The notebook slipped from her fingers and paper flew from the unsnapped rings. Both women bent to retrieve the pages and bumped their heads smartly together. Both women tried to move again, tangled their long legs and fell. They looked at each other in startled amazement and laughed.

Kay, the trek guide, stopped her inventory of the hiking gear long enough to shout over their laughter, "Hey, Jungle Jane. You two are gonna hafta learn to get along a lot better'n that, 'cause I've assigned you two long-legs as tent partners for the rest of the trip."

Ramona managed to swallow the hot words she wanted to hurl at Kay for her thoughtlessly easy nicknaming. Did people never grow up? Instead she managed a smile and said protectively to Jane, "I've sometimes been called Pocahontas."

The sky-blue eyes inspected her from head to foot. The eyes were admiring, and so was the voice. "Of course. Pocahontas was an Indian Princess."

Ramona smiled. "Jungle Jane, I'm sure, is equally such a woman."

Then Ramona noticed Poppy Dillworth, the oldest member of the group of women she'd just been introduced to, cast a curious glance at Kay. But Kay ducked her head and continued checking and sorting the equipment the eight women would need during their trek up the mountain valley.

5

Much To Tell

Jane watched with amusement as Ramona settled all six feet of her length into her sleeping bag. The two women physically filled almost every available space in the little orange tent. At one inch short of six feet herself, Jane had spent a lifetime trying to downscale her large angular body. It felt perversely good to watch someone else struggle for a change.

"So, Ramona, what's *your* reason for signing on for Bwana Bigmouth's Two weeks of Torture?"

Ramona breathed a *whoosh* of capitulation and gave up trying to lie with her elbows above her head. Slanting rays of light from the dying sun splashed on her side of the tent. A warm orange halo glowed behind her head as she turned to speak.

"I wanted some new photographs to use in my artwork . . . and I needed to get out of myself, to be with other people. I . . . you see . . . I . . ." She turned her head and brought the back of her hand to her mouth as if to stop more words from coming out.

Though concerned by her tentmate's evident pain, Jane could not stop enjoying simply looking at Ramona. She had never seen a woman so beautiful and so seemingly unaware of her effect on others. With the orange glow framing her thick dark hair, she might have posed for a painting of an Indian Madonna.

Ramona wore an air of pain and mystery like a carelessly tied cape. She both intrigued and awed Jane, and managed at the same time to appeal to the clown in her. Jane wanted to make her laugh — to chase the sadness from those large, wounded-doe eyes.

When Ramona turned to face Jane again, her eyes glistened. "I'm sorry, Jane. My husband died about two years ago and this is my first venture into the world alone. I'm having a difficult time regaining my balance."

Jane sobered her face appropriately as Ramona continued, "I really thought I was adjusting pretty well — but I think I'm losing it a little. Maybe we could talk about you and *your* reasons for paying Kay good money to torture you for two weeks. Bwana Bigmouth really fits her. How come you call her that?"

25

Jane sat up. "It wasn't hard at all. The first day I saw her at the library handing out flyers, I'd just come in from my mother's farm and I was wearing what *I* thought was surely appropriate clothing for a wilderness trek, my safari shorts, bush jacket and camouflage hat. She looked at my application and back up at me and said — 'Well, well, Jungle Jane, so you think you're tough enough for two weeks in the wilderness.' After that, Bwana Bigmouth just seemed to fit."

Ramona's teeth glinted white in the fading light as she smiled at Jane's story.

Jane's chest filled with a sudden giddy lightness as the force of Ramona's smile washed over her. She wound her long fingers together as she continued, "As far as my reasons for coming on the trip? Well, I'm not exactly sure I know. Since my grandson was born a year ago, I've been restless. Just seemed like a good thing to do with my vacation. I don't know. Middle age crazies maybe?"

Ramona's laughter was welcome as rain to Jane's arid soul. She unconsciously arched her back like a stroked kitten and continued, searching for new ways to bring back Ramona's dazzling smile. "There's not much to tell really, except that somehow I managed to raise two children by myself and never remarried after my husband made himself a dead hero in Vietnam. We'd been separated for a couple of years. He was a man who needed a Stepford wife . . . and I couldn't seem to make myself into that kind of robot. He joined the Marines out of spite, which eventually made my mother very happy. A military widow in the family was certainly more acceptable than a divorcee . . . Really, my life's been pretty ordinary aside from my unreasonable attachment to my cello."

Ramona brightened. "The cello. How wonderful! I play piano for a chamber group in San Antonio. I mean, at least I did before Harold died."

Disappointment filled Jane as Ramona's smile faded.

"Harold was more than just my husband. He was my best friend. We never had children and I'm afraid I was too dependent on his steady presence in my life."

Jane watched helplessly as tears crept down Ramona's cheeks.

"He rescued me from a hard life on the reservation where I boarded with a missionary and his wife. I don't remember my parents, only an old grandfather who died when I was nine. Harold was my shining knight."

Tears flowed freely now, sparkling rivulets in the dying light.

"They called me from California two years ago where he was project manager at a nuclear power plant. He'd suffered a massive coronary and died before they could get him to the hospital."

Ramona rested her chin on her arms atop her raised knees. Her shoulders shook as she cried silently. Jane brushed the tears of sympathy from her own eyes and considered how to respond. Left without her mainstay of sarcasm of humor, she was slow to speak. Finally she laid her hand on Ramona's trembling shoulder, then quickly moved it away and wound her fingers together again.

"I'm so sorry, Ramona. I'm afraid I haven't taken

time to develop friendships outside the closed circle of my family, so I'm rusty at this sort of thing. But I'd be glad to be your friend . . . to help if I can."

Ramona looked up and smiled wistfully, brushing distractedly at the tears. "Thanks," she said and caught her lower lip between her teeth to cut off, it seemed to Jane, something more she might have said.

* * * * *

The next morning Jane won the tenderfoot race to the top of the cliffs along the river. Ramona watched her disappear over the top and abruptly reappear, standing. Jane shaded her eyes with her battered camouflage hat and scanned the valley.

Ramona paid close attention to the arduous task of climbing and pushed herself upward in reckless haste. She handily passed the others, spanning yawning spaces between rocks with graceful, breathtaking leaps. Her long legs still performed the skills she had learned as a girl on the reservation. The sheep had been hers to care for and many times she engineered daring rescues when the curious animals found themselves marooned high on some crag or boxed into a dangerous hole or cave. Ramona reached the top, took Jane's outstretched hand, and allowed herself to be pulled up and over the edge. She shaded her eyes with long fingers and smiled shyly at Jane.

Jane's elbows stuck out from her body in a hands-on-hips scolding-mother pose. "My God, Ramona, you could've killed yourself, you know. I wish I'd had a movie camera on you — all you needed was a sword and you could've auditioned for *Prisoner of Zenda.*"

Ramona thought how grateful she was to Kay for assigning strong, warm, down-to-earth Jane as her buddy for the two weeks they would spend in the mountains. For the first time since Harold's death, Ramona felt the stirrings of something like enthusiasm. She began to pay attention to the world beyond her fingertips.

They watched in silence as the rest of the group groaned into view. First came Desiree Parker and her friend Lu Blassingame, two nurses from Houston in their early thirties. Next came Marcie Judy, a schoolteacher from Austin who hoped to toughen herself up for the rigors she would face as a missionary in South America.

Close behind Marcie came Poppy Dillworth who was, at sixty-five, spryer than might be expected. She thumped her sturdy walking stick on the solid rock like a farmer searching for the ripest melon. *Thock, thock-thock,* she moved up the cliff face. Like a slim, greying wolf, aged and vulnerable, she paled against the vitality and color of the younger women.

Last came their guide Kay Kent and her shadow, Ray Lester, a no-nonsense dance/phys-ed teacher who was Kay's summer partner in the trek business. Ramona and Jane watched as Ray pointed to the black compass watch on her muscular wrist and then said something obviously unkind to Marcie who had fallen behind the others.

Jane turned to Ramona. "I noticed a violin case in Ray's backpack at camp. Do you think it's really a violin, or maybe a submachine gun?"

29

Ramona gave Jane the obligatory chuckle and gazed thoughtfully at the group of women climbing toward their perch.

6

Sisters in the Bushes

The next two days were busy with new activities for Jane. She remembered old skills and tried out new ones with varying degrees of success as the women moved steadily onward up the river valley. She especially enjoyed her growing friendship with Ramona. They talked for hours as they walked and at night after the others were asleep. It seemed to Jane that some emotional dam in Ramona had given way, allowing her to express her grief at losing her husband.

Jane was glad to be able to help. Her supportive nature bloomed under the shower of opportunities afforded it by Ramona's need to talk out her grief and confusion.

The two women squirmed into their sleeping bags in the dark little tent, trying to stretch out the kinks. Both were tired from the earlier adventure of cliff climbing, but that didn't stem the flow of their ongoing exchange of life histories.

Ramona began where she had left off the night before. "You know, Jane — as long as I had Harold, I didn't seem to need many others in my life. I see now I allowed him to insulate me from all the painful things."

"That's not as good as it sounds, is it?" Jane asked.

Ramona gave the idea some consideration. "Maybe not . . . you know, the only problem we ever had was probably our sexual compatibility. Notice I didn't say *in*compatibility. That part of our life dovetailed perfectly. Neither of us really cared much about it. We'd both had unhappy experiences early in life. It was more comfortable for Harold, and for me, after a while, to just forget about it. But now I feel a loss because I've never experienced what all my friends seem to think is the greatest part of woman's life."

Jane sensed Ramona's tension as Ramona raised herself on one elbow in the gloom of the tent. Compassion made Jane's voice louder than usual as she spoke. "You mean you've never had —" She lowered her voice to a throaty whisper at Ramona's quick "Shhhhhhhh."

"You mean you've never had satisfactory sex? Never had an . . . uh . . . never reached . . ." Her voice trailed off, as she found herself somehow unable to say the word. Jane had surprised herself at this response which in some way seemed to suggest that she, Jane, had had satisfactory sex, which was not exactly the truth. Unless you counted masturbation. "I mean, haven't you ever done it yourself?"

"No," Ramona replied, "I think I came close sometimes with Harold but it just never seemed worth the emotional bother to pursue it alone. I feel nervous from time to time and dance by myself until I'm tired or swim pretty hard for a while until I feel more peaceful. I think I've never really *allowed* myself to feel sexually aroused."

Jane thought of all the swimming she herself had done over the years while teaching lifesaving to teenagers. Yeah, that *could* use up a lot of energy, but surely not *that* much.

The atmosphere in the little tent quivered with an intense energy. Jane dimly sensed that an invisible gauntlet had been thrown down at the feet of something struggling steadily forward out of the muck of her own peculiar emotional swamp. A disconcerting buzz of physical excitement flitted through her lower abdomen. She sat up convulsively, bumping her head against the tent. "I think I'll take a little walk in the woods before I go to sleep."

She scooted out of her sleeping bag, carefully maneuvered her tall body through the tiny tent opening and started to walk away, shrugging on her jacket, when the plaintive note of Ramona's, "Hey. Was it something I said?" tugged at her.

She turned and thrust her head back into the

33

tent. "I'm sorry to end this conversation so abruptly, but I think this morning's prunes are beginning to work overtime!"

With the reward of Ramona's soft laughter in her ears she strode quickly toward the woods. She chided herself for once more masking her true feelings by making someone laugh. She reached the protective trees and stepped into the deep shadows thrown by the light of a three-quarter moon. Her cheeks still burned at her unexpected physical response to their intimate conversation.

She skirted the camp, trying to identify the feelings that had caused her abrupt departure from the conversation with Ramona and from the suddenly stifling tent they shared. She kept going back over their talk. Why had she sensed a challenge? To do what? She had felt like saying — Oh, *yeah*? Well, you just *watch* me!

Watch her?

Watch her *what*?

Jane was deep in thought and almost out of the woods into a clearing by the stream when she heard voices and stopped in the shadows. She made out Kay's figure by the way the moonlight gleamed on her pale hair. Kay sprawled on a rock ledge, leaning back with her spraddled knees brought up. Nestled back against her, between her legs, sat Ray. They cuddled with unself-conscious intimacy.

Ohmygod.

In the dark Jane's stomach took a lurch down and over and she stood very still as she realized the two women were lesbians.

Desiree's voice came from just out of Jane's field of sight. "Well, *I'll* bet a week's pay that Jungle Jane

34

and Pocahontas get it on before we leave these mountains."

"*Really*, Desiree!" Lu replied as they both walked into view and sat near Kay and Ray. "There *are* straight women in the world, you know. Honestly! You see a sister behind every bush."

Desiree turned to face Lu in mock seriousness as she replied, "Well, there's probably some truth in that statement. I know I certainly like looking at *your* bush, sister!" She buried her face in the general area of Lu's crotch in a burlesque of loud smacking and licking noises.

Lu slapped Desiree's rear, admonishing her, "Des, honey, control yourself. The others might hear you."

Jane breathed slowly, unconsciously counting a swimmer's count as her mind wrangled with the knowledge that Desiree and Lu were also lesbians and the four of them were discussing the possibility of Jane and Ramona making it a sextet.

Desiree's words fell through the hole where Jane's stomach had been. "*Get it on — Jungle Jane and Pocahontas get it on*" — Desiree had said. She meant sex. Yes, Jane was pretty sure Desiree meant sex, but had she done *anything* to make them think that was a possibility?

Desiree stopped tormenting Lu and raised her head. She fanned her glistening blonde hair across her shoulders as she looked back toward camp. "You guys are playing ostrich. Anyone with half an eye can see big Janey is smitten with our raven-haired, doe-eyed Indian princess. And Pocahontas opens up like a morning glory every time Jane shines that blinding wit in her direction."

Sick with shame, Jane carefully backed out of

hearing distance. She steadied her legs and walked away as briskly as the moonlight would allow. Her mind whirred and cranked with Desiree's accusing remarks.

Well, that was most definitely *not* what had caused her uncomfortable departure from the tent. She just wasn't used to so much forced intimacy with strangers. Ramona needed comforting. It was a natural act to hug someone in pain, wasn't it? Or at least to want to. *Well, wasn't it?*

Maybe if she asked Kay for a new partner . . . *That* would prove Desiree wrong.

But in the meantime she had to return to the tent and sleep a few inches away from Ramona.

Jane sat on a cold rock in the woods long enough to be fairly sure Ramona was asleep. Then she returned to the tent and crawled stealthily into her sleeping bag. She turned her face to the tent wall and spent a restless night punctuated with spells of anguished wakefulness during which she thought about the problem she didn't have.

7

Marcie Finds the Yellow Brick Road

Poppy sat in the tent hunched over a length of
nylon rope. She narrowed her clear blue eyes and
squinted up at Marcie through her trifocals. She
thrust the rope toward Marcie who eyed it as if it
might coil and strike. A sleeping rope-snake at best,
but surely lethal if tortured into a knot.

"Today's lesson is supposed to be a fireman's
knot, Marcie, it's not hard to do. Unless you're

crippled up with arthritis like I am. So stop sniveling and try it again."

"But it *is* hard if you never tied anything but shoestrings."

"Just *do* it, dammit!"

Marcie ran her hand under the strap of her bra, lifting it away from the furrow it made in her soft shoulder, and then busied the pudgy fingers of both hands with the stubborn rope. A tear of frustration escaped and rolled down a freckled cheek.

Marcie seemed achingly young to Poppy, more like twelve than thirty, with her pink tongue held firmly between her teeth as she concentrated on tying the knot. She reminded Poppy of her first lover, Eloise. Dead now these forty years, but still winsomely alive in memory . . . churning through the early morning Brazos river fog in that damned old leaky boat. Plump arms flashing wetly as she shipped the oars to rest and smiled flirtatiously at a much younger, much stronger Poppy.

In fact Eloise was more alive to Poppy than most walking-around people. Poppy dwelt more and more in the long-ago past. The present was duty-laden from dawn until dusk, full of arthritic pain, muscles wearing out and now a damned heart condition which invited fear of dying into the already painful process of living. Every day was just a penance to be somehow endured.

The sunsets of her memory spread the sky of her bleak present with lovely, warm colors and she was loath to leave them to deal with the necessities of daily living. She had grown crusty in language and gruff in demeanor, especially in the past year since her retirement from the Caliche County Sheriff's Department.

With a hawkeyed glance, Poppy took in Marcie's inept struggle with the simple knot. Her short patience snapped its tether and her temper washed over Marcie. "Oh, forever more, you little idiot! How the hell do you think you're gonna survive in a South American jungle? Those savages down there are gonna tie you up and perpetrate unspeakable atrocities on your body anyway because you sure as hell won't be able to untie yourself. Why don't you just stay home where you belong?"

Marcie's dark eyes grew wide and frightened. Tears welled up freely and her lower lip trembled. "You're juh-just r-really *mean,* Poppy. You duh-don't know what will happen to me. You're just trying to scare me." Marcie hugged her knees and bunched up into a quivering ball. Fat tears splashed onto her scuffed Nikes.

A well-deserved dose of remorse propelled Poppy quickly across the small space to wrap her stringy arms around Marcie, to comfort her young tentmate. She was surprised at the feeling of peaceful ease she received from the act.

Marcie buried her head in Poppy's spare bosom and sobbed in earnest as the dam of false courage burst and all her fears cascaded out. Between hiccups and muffled sniffling, Poppy understood a few words.

". . . right, oh Poppy, you're right . . . so scared. Don't want . . . go to . . . merica. Don't have faith God will protect me. I'm just a fake!"

She calmed a little as Poppy gently rocked and crooned to her, murmured comforting, motherly there-there-nows and smoothed her frizzy bronze-colored hair.

Marcie rested her head on Poppy's ropey shoulder and blew her nose on the bandana Poppy offered. Poppy felt a stirring in her chest that had nothing to do with a weak heart. It approximated, she thought, some kind of maternal feeling. She tried to sort it out as Marcie pulled herself together.

I must be getting dotey. All I want to do is climb this mountain one last time and lay down on top and take the long sleep! I don't want to feel like a mother. I'm tired. It's too hard.

Like tying a fireman's knot, huh, Dillworth? You old ass! You mean old shit!

She hugged Marcie tighter as remorse roiled inside her. Marcie sighed and melted against Poppy's dry body like a warm bath.

"You know, Poppy, I never had a mother or grandmother or anything. I mean, I guess I did somewhere. But I'm an orphan and I don't know who they are. I guess it would've felt like this, though. Being hugged, I mean."

"Mmmhmmmm," Poppy murmured, not trusting herself to speak. She was pretty sure the tickly feeling on her cheeks was tears, but it had been years since she had allowed herself that luxury. Even thoughts of her coming death did not bring tears. Life was damn perverse, that's what.

Sometimes the dragon wins, Dillworth, you worn out Don Quixote. Sometimes the fire-breathing, foul-smelling, scaly old bastard of a dragon wins! . . . and there ain't nothing you can do about it except just slide on down the castle wall.

Poppy's inner dialogue stopped its clamor as

Marcie made tentative moves to extricate herself from Poppy's fierce hug. "Thanks for lettin' me blubber, Poppy."

Poppy averted her eyes, always embarrassed about showing feelings. "Well, I think it was my fault, I was pretty rough on you. Don't know what gets into me sometimes. Maybe Desiree's right about me. Maybe I've just gotten old and mean. A condition of the heart, as she says."

"How long have you known Desiree, Poppy?"

"About ten years, now. Ever since they graduated from nurses' training." Poppy mentally chomped her lip as the "they" slipped out.

"You mean her and Lu, don't you?" Marcie flickered brown eyes shyly at Poppy, trying to put her next question into words. "Have Desiree and Lu been best friends all this time? Why hasn't either one of them gotten married? They're both real good looking . . . especially Desiree. She looks like a movie star."

Poppy briefly considered telling Marcie that they *were* married — to each other — but decided instead to pose a question and let Marcie draw her own conclusions.

"Well . . . what do *you* think, Ladybug?"

Marcie's cheeks flattened under the weight of an obviously startling insight. Her eyes widened and she stammered, "Oh. Oh *my*."

Poppy grinned at her mischievously. "If you ask is this still Kansas, Toto or call me Auntie Em, I'm not gonna answer any more questions."

Marcie apparently had about a thousand more questions, but she shut her gaping mouth. Poppy watched with amusement as she unconsciously tugged

41

again at the errant bra strap and turned to the task of readying her equipment for the day's hike up the river.

* * * * *

Kay knocked ceremoniously on the tent pole, clattering the underside of her ring against the metal. "Can I see you women for a minute?"

Puzzled, Poppy and Marcie crawled out of the tent and stood blinking in the early morning sunlight.

"Jane wants to swap buddies for the rest of the trip," Kay said.

Poppy's left eyebrow shot up her forehead and quivered there, holding up ropes of wrinkles as she raised the right brow in a parody of unspoken questions. Kay shook her head slowly and shrugged her shoulders at Poppy.

Marcie, still reeling from her earlier enlightenment, did not seem up to unravelling the knotty little nuances of meaning passing between the other two women. Desiree and Lu had just come into view and Marcie's attention was riveted on Desiree, whose tawny, leonine beauty loudly invited attention. Her long legs encased in skin-tight, electric purple Spandex reflected undulating flashes of sunlight. She performed limbering up exercises while she walked in front of Lu.

"Let's flip a coin, Marcie," Poppy suggested, although she did not intend to lose this chance to talk at length to Ramona. "The loser gets Jungle Jane."

Desiree rolled her dramatic green eyes in exaggerated disbelief. "My God," she said. "If that

42

doll is second prize, what does the winner get, Rita Mae Brown and a thousand bucks a day for life?"

"Put a lid on it, Des!" Lu exclaimed as she dragged the snickering Desiree toward the woods.

Poppy darted a concerned glance at Marcie who looked as if the Munchkins had just nuked Emerald City.

8

Jane Wimps Out

"I asked Kay if I could switch partners so I can get to know as many different people as possible while we're on the trek." Jane kept her guilty blue eyes busily involved with the buckles and snaps of her backpack while she talked.

Hot tears filled Ramona's eyes as Jane's announcement sunk in. She felt naked, vulnerable. Then, in rapid succession, embarrassed and angry. She trembled as adrenalin-induced nausea choked off the question at her lips. She turned abruptly and stalked away.

Good God! She felt like a gangly reservation teenager again, snubbed by the townies. She fought to slow her long legs to a walk. She wanted to run, full-out, up the canyon and shout down her own raging echo as she'd done as a girl when the pain was too much to bear.

Her present pain seemed all out of proportion to the facts, though. So Jane had asked for a new partner. So what.

In her need to unload so much emotional baggage, she must have overstepped some boundary of good taste. She didn't for a minute believe the cockamamie reason Jane gave for wanting a new buddy. Ramona was sure it was something *she* had done.

She was furious with herself for allowing "Sky-eyes" inside her defenses. She must be getting soft, or old, or *something*, to think she could have a real friend. Someone she could really share with.

Okay! No more sharing secrets, no more trust, no more *anything*. She had photographs to take, anyway. She slung her camera case savagely against her hip, punching a bruise in the process. Her eyes teared at the sudden physical pain, but at least it was something she could deal with. She knew why her hip hurt. The tightness in her throat was something else again.

All that day, she lagged behind the others and threw herself vehemently into recording on film everything that even remotely held the possibility of being turned into a painting. She put on her sunglasses, pulled her hat down over her eyes and dashed about setting up and removing tripods, meters and equipment like a veritable Ansel Adams.

9

Ramona Takes a Tumble and Jane Dives In

Jane walked downstream until she found a place where she could climb down close to the river that rushed and tumbled then stilled as it curved past a bend under the cliffs atop which the women were camped. The farther they had come into the mountains the more savage the river had become. Soon they would leave it behind and strike out upland.

She picked her way back along the river until she

was directly below camp. An inviting flat-topped boulder jutted out over the deep green water. She reached the outer edge of it, lay face down and let her gaze rest lightly on the eddying pools close to the base of the cliff.

Sparkles of light between the cliff and her boulder caught her eye. She inched closer and discovered a beautiful, symmetrical spider web stretched close to the water. As she watched, entranced, the web came to life and twinkling sparklets of water flew as the web's architect danced deftly into its center and swayed motionless for a frozen moment, then startled Jane by springing toward her to seize a hapless moth that fluttered against its prison.

Her mind went back to the scene in camp that had prompted her solitary escape. Desiree and Marcie had been engaged in a joking struggle to place kindling in the correct fashion to lay a proper fire. She had watched the star-struck Marcie bumble into Desiree's web of eroticism just as surely as the moth below her lay encased now in silken bindings. Desiree's teasing yet somehow predatory behavior toward Marcie had disgusted her. It confused Jane that anyone as spiteful as Desiree could be successful as a nurse. A profession for a compassionate *caregiver,* surely.

Her stomach churned with conflicting emotions. Since her discovery that the woods were full of lesbians, she'd had very little peace of mind.

Jane felt badly that Ramona was hurt and angry at her sudden withdrawal from their friendship, but it was best for them both. And she *couldn't* tell Ramona the *real* reason she had wanted to change buddies:

48

that the others were making book on their innocent friendship growing into much more.

But she *missed* Ramona. It cut her like a cold wind every time she saw her — heard her voice, her laugh, was stunned by her sunburst of a smile.

Jane turned over on the rock and watched a small cloud creep past the edge of the cliff. Her hand found a piece of driftwood upon which she unconsciously fingered the F minor arpeggio that was giving her so much trouble in the Dvorak.

Almost as if in response to Jane's churning thoughts, Ramona appeared on the lip of the cliff above — silhouetted against the cloud. Jane watched as she stationed a tripod perilously close to the edge and moved with fluid dancer's grace as she sighted through the camera lens toward the distant hills. Jane closed her eyes hoping to still the buzz that crept from behind her knees and along her inner thighs, but it did no good. Ramona's tall figure was outlined in fiery orange negative against the inside of Jane's eyelids.

At the sound of a shout she opened her eyes and what she saw caused her heart to leap in horror as Ramona lost her footing and pitched forward in a sickening fall toward the river.

Ohgodno!

Jane clutched her chest and scrambled quickly to her feet. She paused long enough to catch sight of Ramona flailing wildly against the rushing current, then she dived up and outward in a graceful, efficient arc and sliced into the roiling water below.

Her heart pounded as she came up for air, slashing powerful strokes in a steady line toward the diamond white flash of Ramona's scarf.

Where was that woman anyway? Why didn't she stay on the top of the water? There! A flash of wet face. Dark hair billowed out around Ramona's head, fanned by the fast current.

Under! Goddam. She went under!

Jane sucked in air and pushed herself down into the icy stream. Her hand touched the threadlike pull of Ramona's hair as she swirled past her. Her fingers closed convulsively and grasped a handful of it.

I've got her!

Jane fought to the top of the churning water. She drew Ramona's limp body along with her. She grasped her arm, turned her, reached across her chest and pulled Ramona's head above the surface.

She carefully placed her strokes, floating efficiently, using the eddying force of the water to avoid the rocks that rose crazily from the river bed.

She struggled to bring them over to a flat rock ledge at the river's bank. A steady low roaring pressed her ears.

The falls!

How close were they?

She scissored her long legs savagely, closing the distance to the edge of the rock. The current threw them against a pile of dead trees and the force of the water held them there. Jane clenched her teeth against the tremor of the falls as she pulled back against the current alongside the trees. Her right foot connected painfully with the lower edge of the rock.

Her leg bones thrummed with the vibrating power of the falls as she moved steadily out of the water. The river lost its hold on them as Jane broke out of the current and dragged Ramona onto the warm dry rock.

50

Her stomach tightened with dread. She turned Ramona face down and chanted rhythmically as she pushed down against her ribcage. "Oh God . . . not dead . . . please . . . not dead . . . Oh God."

Ramona's back muscles contracted in a spasm as she coughed, sputtered, and then took hungry gulps of air. Jane sagged with relief as Ramona struggled to sit up, pulling hair away from her face.

Ramona's dark eyes widened with mingled fear and gratitude. She smiled thinly and tried to speak to Jane over the furious roar of the falls. Jane's chest expanded in reckless joy at knowing Ramona was all right. She tried not to see Ramona's full beautiful breasts, outlined by her wet shirt. Conflicting desires swelled mightily within Jane as she sat motionless, close — so close — to her frightened friend.

Without willing it to happen, it just did. Jane pulled Ramona to her, held her tightly, rocking back and forth. She kissed the water away from Ramona's face and wet it with her tears at the same time. Ramona clung to her rescuer like a frightened child. Jane felt the clamorous beating of Ramona's heart merge with the pounding of the falling water.

They embraced, suspended in the noisy tumult. The only real thing in the world was the touch of their bodies. Jane's comforting kisses brushed Ramona's lips and her heart leaped as Ramona responded passionately. Her full mouth quested, her lips moved hungrily against Jane's. Her tongue darted quickly into Jane's mouth, searching for and finding Jane's tongue.

Jane's brain took urgent direction from the lower half of her body. She responded to Ramona's need with an answering need of her own.

51

The two women kissed in pure celebration of being safe and alive. Then their embrace quickened with raw passion. They lay back on the sun-warmed rock and held each other tighter, lost in a roaring, warm-wet world.

Jane came to her senses first and pulled herself roughly away. Ramona lay almost in a swoon. Even if they screamed at each other they couldn't hear . . . and what would they say? *I'm sorry, it must have been something in the water?*

Ramona opened her eyes and looked up at Jane with a whole universe of surprised understanding on her face.

Jane looked at her feet, at the river, at the sky. Everywhere except at the woman whose kiss had made her feel like raw electrical current was coursing through her. The blue-hot ache in her groin rose in warm waves up her body and her cheeks flamed in an agony of embarrassment. She put her hands to her face and, like a child, peered through her fingers at Ramona who sat transfixed.

Ramona smiled and shook her head, as if to clear it. A flush of confusion reddened her face when she realized Jane wasn't smiling.

Jane won her struggle for inner control. She signalled to Ramona they must get back to camp.

She shouted through cupped hands into Ramona's ear, "Can you make the walk?"

Ramona nodded weakly. They began the exhausting climb away from the river and up through the rocks. Jane turned once to help Ramona up a particularly steep incline and winced guiltily as Ramona grasped her proffered arm.

Ramona regarded Jane quizzically, with hurt dark

eyes. She caught her trembling lower lip in her teeth. Emotions and feelings she had never before experienced flashed through her like timed fireworks. The flames of first passion leaped unchecked through her body.

Behind it all, steely-thin threads of insight wove a pattern of resolve around Ramona's hammering heart.

10

The Big 'L' Word

That evening, after everyone finally stopped talking about the adventure of Jane's daring rescue, Kay, Ray, Desiree and Lu took an after-dinner stroll. Poppy tossed her gear into the tent with Ramona's and tried to talk to her new buddy.

She shot her first question like an arrow into Ramona's melancholy. "How come Jungle Jane wanted to switch buddies? What's her major maladjustment, anyway? You gals fight over whose feet got stuck out in the cold?" Poppy quizzed Ramona, intent on discovering what had caused the rift between the two women.

Ramona turned away, but not before Poppy caught the glint of tears.

"Oops. Didn't mean to hit a nerve," Poppy began, but snapped her mouth shut as Ramona squared her shoulders and continued to look out across the mountain meadow. Her eyes were fixed on some invisible planet, light years away from the subject of Jane Mary Jackson and any maladjustment *she* might have. Major or minor.

"Ramona," Poppy mused for a moment, then tried another tack. "The study of American Indian cultures is a hobby of mine. Can I ask you a few questions?"

Ramona turned to face Poppy, her expression one of polite interest. "Sure, Poppy. I may not be much help, but I'll do my best."

"I'm interested in the belief that each person had the right to end their earthly stay when they felt their usefulness was over. Do you have any knowledge of that custom?" Poppy self-consciously fingered the single bear claw that had bounced against her spare chest every day of the past four years since Irma's death.

The barest hint of a smile played at the corners of Ramona's mouth as she answered. "Except for having seen Dustin Hoffman in the movie *Little Big Man,* I'm afraid I probably know less than you do. I was brought up mostly by missionaries who were pretty successful in replacing my early memories with their own Christian beliefs. Besides, I left the reservation quite early . . . and I've lived a very different life since."

Poppy could do little except nod and try once more to find a subject for conversation. "I've noticed you taking pictures. Are you a shutterbug, or is it just a novel way to get to swim in the river?" Poppy knew she was taking a chance, but Ramona's reticence was beginning to annoy her.

She knew by Ramona's quick intake of air she was right on target. "Wait," Poppy said. She caught Ramona's elbow as she tried to move away. "I think I can help. I believe I've figured out what's bothering Janey."

Ramona's eyes were filled with raw anguish and confusion. Poppy watched her defenses crumble as Ramona sagged and sat cross-legged, holding her face in her hands.

"Oh, Poppy. What could you say that would possibly explain Jane's behavior?"

Poppy removed her glasses, breathed on the lenses and wiped them clean with a faded purple bandana, stalling for time as she considered how to make good on her promise of help. She finally wedged the meticulously cleaned glasses atop her white hair, aviator style, sat gingerly on the spread blanket and took Ramona's hand. "I'll begin by telling you my own story. You're a smart girl — you'll put it rightly together as I go along. You can stop me with questions whenever you feel like it."

Ramona nodded and tucked a few straying wisps of hair back into the bun at the nape of her neck as Poppy began to speak.

"I was born in Brush Arbor, Texas, and I was a child of the Great Depression. The summer I was nine, my mama and baby brother and me went to Maine to live with Mama's brother on his potato farm. There was no money to be had so we worked his potato fields for our room and board."

Poppy absently re-cleaned her glasses as she warmed to her tale. "We children were closer to the ground, so squatting and crawling was easier on us than the grownups. We'd been set to do the dirty job of picking the freshly dug spuds out of the clods. We rubbed them off and filled bags that stood open between the rows.

"One particular day is fixed in my memory like a new-minted coin. I spied a cloud of dust across the fields by the railroad trestle. I got excited because only someone rich and important would be driving something big enough to make that much dust. And make it that fast!

"We all stood still and shaded our eyes to watch a large grey roadster come to a sliding stop by the wagons. A very tall woman got out and hallooed at us — waved her hat and slapped it against the wagon to knock loose the dust. A shorter stout woman came around to join her and they stood there waiting for us to come over and talk to them."

"Who were they, Poppy?" Ramona was fascinated.

"I'm getting to that, Ladybug." Poppy stood, bent at the waist and pulled her red hiking socks up as far as they would go. She sat again with her legs straight out in front of her, tested her weight against the tent pole and leaned back. "Well, since I was the closest to the wagons and because I was a fearless, curious child — I ran as fast as my legs would take me and fell, all wadded up in a raggedy, dirty little heap, right up against the tall lady's feet. She knelt and gathered me up in arms as strong as my uncle's. Plumb ruined her white traveling clothes. She sat me up on the wagon seat, exclaiming 'Are you hurt?' I shook my head no so hard my straw hat untied and my pigtails came flapping out.

" 'Oh, Hick, darling — look — she's a little *girl*,' the tall one said. The fat woman grinned and took out her notebook and started writing.

"My uncle and the rest of the grown-ups had all gathered up by then and my mama stood by me and patted my leg. The tall lady introduced herself and my uncle said he reckoned the First Lady didn't have to tell a bunch of Democrats who *she* was. She asked a lot of questions about how the crops and prices were and what did they want their President to do for them?

"She also introduced 'Hick Darling' as her friend, a reporter and traveling companion.

"They didn't stay long — but it was plenty long enough for me to fix in my heart and mind the picture of two strong women — women who *did* things who made a *difference*! I swore I would grow up and find me a companion like 'Hick Darling' had. And I did, too. I've outlived two of the best women the Goddess ever saw fit to place on this Mother Planet!"

Poppy's voice had risen until she was a little breathless. She stopped speaking and raised eloquent eyebrows at her troubled listener. "Well," she said, softer now, "any questions yet?"

Ramona's mobile face reflected her insights too well. She blinked and busied herself with a piece of loose thread on the toe of her hiking boot.

"Do you know what I'm trying to say, Ramona?" Poppy asked gently.

Ramona raised her eyes and nodded.

Poppy continued, "I think your friend Janey has been frightened to death by the big 'L' word, honey."

"The big *el* word? . . . Oh." Ramona ducked her head again as she mentally put the rest of the letters together. She sat very still. Poppy noted, with a bit of well-hidden amusement, that even the semi-darkness could not hide the blush that spread up Ramona's cheeks.

*   *   *   *   *

Desiree, Lu, Kay and Ray returned from their moonlight walk and approached the two women seated on the blanket.

"Telling ghost stories, Poppy? Or just some juicy fairy tales?" Desiree teased Poppy as she plopped herself on the blanket beside the older woman. "Is this just a one-on-one pow-wow, or can anyone join?"

Ramona straightened her back and hugged her midsection as the other three women found places and formed a loose circle. She threw Poppy an apprehensive look that Poppy read as a plea to keep the subject of their conversation secret.

Poppy braced herself as Desiree tossed her hair back away from her face and prepared to speak to Ramona. Lu unobtrusively pincered Desiree's knee between her strong thumb and forefinger. But Desiree could not resist teasing Ramona — even though Lu's knuckles whitened as she dug her fingers under the tendon in Desiree's leg.

"What's Jungle Jane's deal? Doesn't she know about the ole Injun custom that says if you save someone's life you're responsible for them forever after?"

59

She winced as Lu dug into her knee. But she kept her eyes on Ramona, who had brought her head up sharply at Desiree's insistent meddling.

The color drained from Ramona's cheeks as she answered. "I believe it is also customary for enemies to paint themselves for war and not present themselves as friends. I'm very tired, please excuse me." Ramona rose stiff-backed and walked regally away from the group of women.

Lu was first to react. She jumped upright, her eyes blazed fiercely. "That's *it,* Des. This time you've gone too far. You've got the sensitivity of an iguana. Just who the hell do you think you are, anyhow?" She jammed her clenched fists into the pockets of her denim jacket and stalked away.

Kay said quickly, "I think it's probably time for us to turn in, too. Big day tomorrow. We have a long hike to reach halfway point." She and Ray left quietly, leaving Poppy and Desiree alone on the blanket in front of the tent.

Poppy cleared her throat and waited for Desiree to speak. Desiree stared into the darkness in the direction Lu had taken, then tented her slender fingers, nervously bending and clicking one long lacquered thumbnail against the other. Poppy saw the unmistakable sparkle of a tear as Desiree glanced quickly at her, then away before she picked up a twig and slapped it sharply against her shoe.

"Ah, shit, Poppy," she said finally and stared morosely at her feet.

"Well, m'dear, tell me something, will you?"

Desiree stopped slapping her shoe and looked up at Poppy.

"What in the blue-eyed world are you so angry at

all the time? What makes you so goddam vicious, honey?"

"I really don't know, Pops."

"I think you better figure it out. Things don't seem too good between you and Lu just now. Being beautiful gives you a lot of power but you can't misuse it like you've been doing. In all the time I've known you two, that's the first time I've ever seen Lu lose her cool at you."

"And heaven knows, she's had cause, hunh Pops? . . ."

Poppy didn't answer. Desiree looked down and resumed punishing her shoe. Her shoulders suddenly drooped. She threw the stick into the darkness, wrapped her arms around her knees and rocked back and forth, silently crying.

"Ah, shit, Pops," she repeated bleakly and met Poppy's gaze. Mascara ran down her cheeks and Poppy stifled an impulse to point out how much it looked like war paint.

"What am I gonna do now?"

Poppy recognized true contrition in Desiree's face and voice. "I think you might start out by making friends with Ramona. If you can pull that off, honey . . . then Lu'll come around on her own."

11

Peace Offering

Morning mist rose from far below the hikers and sneaked its way up ravines and into valleys where smaller streams flowed down to join the river. A craggy green-black conifer stood sentinel on a high point. Ramona lagged behind the others to photograph it, then shouldered her pack and equipment and jogged to catch up again. She slowed her step warily as she glimpsed the solitary figure of a woman through the trees ahead. She set her jaw as the figure turned and she saw it was Desiree.

Ramona stopped and stood for a moment, observing Desiree who sat on a rock, hugging her knees and cradling her head dejectedly in the crook of one arm. Her usually loose and flowing blonde hair was caught back severely from her face with a scarf tied round in back. Her orange backpack stood propped against the rock and she slowly tapped it with a slim green book she held in one hand. Ramona took a deep breath, tensed her shoulders and stepped into view.

Desiree slid from the rock and stood awkwardly waiting for her to cover the short distance between them. "Uh, hi, Ramona," she said. "I want to offer you an apology."

Ramona stared at the ground and struggled with a strong impulse to tell her to go straight to hell and stay there. Her gaze traveled up Desiree's body until their eyes met. She was shocked to see Desiree wore no makeup this morning. A faint spray of freckles marched across her nose while her red-rimmed eyes spoke of recent crying.

Ramona reluctantly yielded to the raw-edged plea in Desiree's voice and to the unspoken appeal in her green eyes. She shrugged out of her backpack and leaned it against the rock beside Desiree's.

Desiree stammered uncharacteristically. "I . . . I . . . I mean." She stopped, fidgeted, began again. "You . . . well, what I . . . what I'm . . . Ah, shit, Ramona. I'm trying to say I'm sorry, but I must sound like an idiot!"

Ramona smiled and offered her hand as Desiree

chewed one half of her lower lip and twisted the book she held.

"OK. We'll start over. Apology accepted."

Desiree squeezed Ramona's hand as Ramona gestured toward the book Desiree had clamped under her arm.

"That book must be pretty good to distract you from all this beautiful scenery."

Desiree looked around her and then back at the book in her hand. "Oh, no. I mean yes . . . I mean — it's a very good book but I read it years ago and sometimes I read it again. It's sort of a peace offering. I want you to have it."

She hesitated for a second and Ramona thought she caught a tiny spark of mischief in her eyes.

"I think it'll help you understand some things. Especially about Janey." Desiree held out the book.

Ramona took it, busied her eyes with the title and then opened it. She read silently through tears that had sprung up at the mention of Jane's name. *Curious Wine* by Katherine V. Forrest. Words from the blurbs on the first page caused Ramona's heart to thunder. ". . . *ultimate lesbian love novel . . . two beautiful women discovering themselves and each other.*"

She closed the book and leaned against the rock to relieve her trembling knees. Her face warmed with acute embarrassment. She looked at Desiree.

"My God. Does *everyone* know? Is it *that* obvious?"

Desiree moved closer and hugged Ramona's broad shoulders. "It might not be obvious to straight women." She released Ramona and moved around to face her. "But most — ahem — if not all of us on this trip are lesbians."

"You mean you and . . ."

"Yeah, honey, me and Lu. *And* Kay and Ray. *And* Poppy. And probably Marcie — one of these days. Only the Goddess knows for sure about you and Janey. But that little book'll help you figure it all out."

Ramona struggled with the sudden need to laugh and cry and shout all at the same time. All these other women! How wonderful. And how *terrible.* Something deep inside her that had begun to grow when she and Jane kissed by the waterfall, some new and wonderful life-spark now raced around the rings of an ever-expanding upward spiral. Up from her vagina, and through her abdomen to flit about her stomach and settle finally in her ribcage — zipping around like a wasp inside a hot lamp globe.

Desiree stood her backpack on the rock, placed Ramona's hand on it to steady it, turned and laced her arms through the straps. She groaned at the weight and shifted it for maximum comfort. "Read the book, honey," she said as she turned to walk away, ". . . then we'll talk tonight. I've got some ideas how you can get Jane's mind off the jungle — if you know what I mean."

Ramona nodded. Grateful to Desiree for knowing she needed some time alone, she watched her stride away up the trail. Something about the way she walked reminded Ramona of a camel finding its center of gravity under a heavy saddle. She chuckled and looked down at the book in her hand. It fell easily open to page ninety-one where a corner had been turned down.

She began to read.

Minutes later, her heart pounded a tattoo as she absentmindedly shouldered her pack, never missing a sentence, and ambled up the trail — turning pages as she climbed.

She finished the chapter in a rush of emotion and physical heat. Her groin throbbed and her panties were damp between her long legs. She closed the book, placed it carefully in her pack, leaned her head back and let out a wild whoop that echoed up the valley.

Then she ran. She stretched her legs out in great strides, pumping her arms. She pushed her body hard while her mind raced ahead even faster to the coming evening when they reached the halfway camp and Desiree would reveal her plan.

12

Halfway There

The group of women left the river valley behind them early in the day. They had climbed steadily since morning. Kay urged them on over seldom used trails. At last they tramped through the cool shade of tall pines and out onto a meadow. A sparkling stream divided the grassy clearing and gurgled down beside an outcropping of slab-sided boulders that protected the edge of the campsite.

Kay faced the women who had all sat or fallen to

the ground, moaning and shedding their packs. "All right women. We've made it. This is halfway point. We came here for four days. Y'all know what to do, so get on your feet and get to it!"

Jane said to Marcie under her breath, "Bwana Bigmouth make natives *restless.*"

Marcie giggled as she struggled to her feet.

The women rapidly applied their newly acquired knowledge and set up tents, constructed a fire pit and marked off the latrine area. Kay uncovered a cache of canned goods she had stashed earlier in the year. Soon tantalizing cooking smells wafted on the swiftly cooling evening air: steaming coffee, savory chili full of tender pasta shells, and chocolate pudding for dessert. They ate with gusto and no one complained when Kay suggested they turn in early.

Though Jane was exhausted, sleep did not come immediately. She'd noticed with some puzzlement that Ramona and Desiree had had their heads together during supper and that Ramona's cheeks glowed with high color. Her throaty laugh had curled inside Jane's ear like a soft caress. She forced her thoughts away from Ramona and quelled the feelings that began to vie for equal time with the chocolate pudding in her stomach. Despite her aching muscles and tired body, Jane lay awake, struggling to free her mind and body from the searing memory of their kiss by the waterfall.

Surely it had been only a natural extension of the high emotion of the rescue. She filled her mind with thoughts of her family back home: her grandson, her job, the fall music season and the Dvorak concerto she had to rehearse — all those pleasantly familiar parts of her life she would soon return to. The events of this trek were only a bizarre episode to be left behind in another week. She forced her mind to work through the intricacies of the glissando just after the opening phases of the adagio.

Jane fell asleep finally and dreamed of being late for work and having nothing to wear but a grass skirt that came open when she walked and exposed her naked vulva.

* * * * *

The next morning Jane awoke later than the others and to her dismay was last in line for the "shower." The small stream formed a falls where it cascaded over the rocks just down from the large boulders at the edge of camp. Bushes and tree limbs around the natural stair down to the pool where the falls culminated blossomed with colorful towels, washcloths and articles of clothing drying in the sun.

Jane gathered her laundry and headed for the shower, bypassing the bench by the firepit where Desiree sat drying her hair, in close conversation again with Ramona. Jane's breath caught in her throat as Ramona looked back over her shoulder and met Jane's eyes evenly. Ramona lowered her long lashes, looked slowly up again and smiled.

Jane forced her legs to move toward the edge of the clearing, away from the stabbing beauty of Ramona's smile. And away from the tinkling sound of Desiree's soft laughter.

"Hey, Jane! Wait up — you lost something."

Yeah . . . my mind . . . I lost my goddam mind!

Marcie caught up with her and handed her a pair of pink panties. Jane blushed so hard it hurt her sunburn.

She quickly made her way down to the pool, peeled out of her grey *Dallas Symphonia 10K Run* sweatshirt and pants, and welcomed the icy shock of the cold water on her burning skin.

Marcie appeared at the edge of the pool. "What're you gonna do for the solstice celebration tonight?"

"What kind of celebration?" Jane shouted as she toweled the water from her ears.

"Solstice. You know. The longest day of the year . . . and then the days start getting shorter again. Lu just told us the moon'll be full tomorrow and it'll be a perfect time to make a celebration and prepare for our survival hike."

"But what do you mean, *do* for the celebration?"

"Ray's gonna play her violin, Poppy has a little drum and she's gonna do Indian chants. Desiree's keeping hers a secret. Kay plays a wooden flute-whistle . . . I don't know what I'm gonna do, yet."

Marcie stared into the distance, thoughtful. "Oh yeah — Lu's gonna 'facilitate the circle' and ask Mother Earth's blessing for our hike tomorrow and Ramona said since she didn't think to bring her piano — she'll do a dance to Ray's violin."

Jane pounded and wrung the water from her laundry with more force than necessary. So that was what Ramona and Desiree had been cooking up. Yeah — a cello would've also been difficult to wag up the mountain. But what else could she offer? Well, she had the whole day to think about it. She'd come up with something.

* * * * *

The camp hummed all day with activity. Occasional sounds of music or drumming mixed with hoots and catcalls, and ever-present laughter echoed through the trees and across the meadow. Jane was delighted to find a rambling vine of gourds covering a fallen tree by the stream. She knew immediately what her contribution to the celebration would be. She spent most of the rest of the morning scouting the woods for pine cones, seeds, and round pebbles from the stream. She filled her pockets and her hat with anything that appealed to her and spent the afternoon alone at the edge of the clearing shooing away anyone who came too close. She sat cross-legged and carved, whittled, tied and whacked in furious industry.

13

Me? Jane?

Excitement ran high as evening neared and the smoky pink disk of the sun dipped behind the line of rocks. Behind the women, as if right on cue, the orange moon appeared through the trees and they quieted in response to the magical moment nature had bestowed on their high-spirited celebration.

Chills ran up Jane's neck as Poppy drummed softly, accompanied by the high haunting sound of Kay's flute. Lu stepped in the direction of the setting sun with her arms outstretched in supplication. Her voice rang clear and sweet as she addressed Grandmother Sun, Mother Moon and all the Directions. The women all stood, joined hands and formed a circle around the glowing fire. All the women chanted except Ramona, Marcie and Jane.

"The Ear-rth is our Mo-other, we must take care of her."

How wonderful, Jane thought, to feel the validation deep within, of women's voices praising earth as their mother. A new emotion welled in her chest — like pride, a sudden bloom of self-esteem, a good feeling she would seek again.

The women's voices still echoed down the valley as Lu began to speak. She remained standing while the others settled onto blankets.

"In the past few years I have become aware of the herstory of women's spirituality. In antiquity we were priestesses and leaders of the world community, respected and revered. Our celebration tonight honors the female power of the universe. We are gathered to celebrate that power in ourselves, in each other and in our Mother — the Earth."

She smile, clasped her hands together and then extended them palms-up toward the others. "Who comes as first giver?"

Jane surprised them all by jumping to her feet. "I play cello," she began. "But as it's been remarked, it would be difficult to stuff it in a backpack . . . so instead I made you all something with my trusty jungle machete."

She withdrew a small hunting knife from the scabbard on her belt and looked pointedly at Kay. She jigged her eyebrows and got a laugh for acknowledging her status as Jungle Jane. "I've utilized some ancient scout-leader skills and made each of you a memento of our wilderness journey. A trek-rattle. I've carved a design on the gourds representing my observations about each of you." She moved around the circle, giving each woman her gift.

Kay burst into laughter as she held hers up for the others to see. Jane had incised a pith helmet atop a face with a huge open mouth.

Ray's depicted a violin bowed by a long stemmed flower. Ray shyly turned it so the others could see it. She seemed a little embarrassed but smiled widely at Jane in appreciation.

Lu's gourd was covered with designs suggesting the phases of the moon and many five-pointed stars. Lu looked at Jane with teary eyes and held the rattle close to her chest.

Marcie blinked at hers. A large open eye stared back at her. She looked quizzically at Jane. Jane leaned close and said, "You came on this trek to firm up the vision of your future. It's to help you see better." Marcie smiled, ducked her head and mumbled thank-you sounds.

Jane stopped in front of Desiree and paused mischievously before she offered her her gift. Desiree took it and turned it toward the light of the fire. She arched an eyebrow then broke into a grin as she figured out what it was. She held it up to quiet the chorus of, "What is it — we wanna see."

"I think it's a magic wand." She looked at Jane, who nodded confirmation. Desiree's eyebrow went up again as she laughed and said, "I guess it means Jane thinks I'm either a fairy godmother or the tooth fairy."

Or a misguided, meddling Tinkerbell . . . Jane thought happily as she turned to Poppy and spoke. "I've noticed you wear a bear claw around your neck. I was going to carve a bear on your rattle — but every time I tried to think how a bear looks, the image of this huge old turtle would pop into my thoughts. So I decided it must hold some special meaning for you."

Poppy blanched and stared at the rattle as if it might come to life. Cords stood out in her slender, graceful neck as she stood and grasped Jane's arm. "That old turtle is my power animal. She's very important to me, indeed. *Very* important . . . thank you, Jane." Poppy shook the rattle, listening with obvious pleasure to its sounds. She surprised Jane by hugging her hard and then by sitting back on her blanket and staring tight-lipped into the fire.

Jane's heart thudded as she turned to face Ramona, who looked up at her from eyes as dark and full as the night around them. "I've made an Indian sign for our Pocahontas." She tried to speak lightly, to the group at large . . . but every cell in her body was magnetized in Ramona's direction. She tore herself away and returned to her seat as Ramona held up her rattle for the others to view. A stylized cloud with a straight bottom covered the large end of the gourd. A jagged bolt of lightning emerged from it and traveled down the handle.

Desiree poked Ramona playfully, raised her eyebrows and rolled her eyes in Jane's direction, the meaning of which was not lost on Jane. Her heart leaped with relief when Lu rose quickly and spoke.

"Thank you, Jane. What marvelous gifts. I'm sure I speak for every woman here when I tell you they

75

will be cherished." A general murmur of assent mingled with the vigorous sound of shaking rattles as she continued, "Now who's next?"

All eyes turned to Poppy as she began a familiar shuffle-step rhythm on her drum. The *swish-ka* . . . *swish-ka* voices of the women's rattles joined Poppy's drumbeat.

Poppy swayed trance-like with her eyes closed and sang softly. Her powerful old-woman voice, low and gravel-throated, pulled a net of goosebumps over Jane's body and tears from her eyes. The almost-but-not-quite words of Poppy's plaintive song filled the camp and echoed down the steep valley. She held up her hands to stop the rattles, tilted her head back and sang the last shrill notes to the rising moon. As the echo died into silence the distant *skreee* of a hawk sounded as if in answer to the song.

Poppy nodded her head at the hawk's call and sat back, still and quiet with her head bowed, her profile O'Keeffe-esque in the moonlight.

Jane looked around the circle. No one seemed willing to break the spell of the chant. They remained silent and thoughtful until Lu rose and turned to face Poppy.

"That was magnificent, Poppy. Thank you for sharing part of your old folks ceremony with us."

Poppy raised her head at Lu's last words and blinked her blue eyes open wide like a sleepy terrapin who'd suddenly become alert and aware of close company.

Lu turned again to face the others, arms out, palms-up. "And who is next?"

Desiree cleared her throat dramatically and stood.

On her cue, Lu and Kay and Ray — evidently well-rehearsed — hummed the schmaltzy melody employed by most amateur magicians.

From her backpack Desiree pulled a plastic milk jug filled with a dark liquid and held it high, for everyone to see. "Tah-dahhhh!"

With a grand flourish she next produced a stack of paper cups and began to fill them, to a chorus of hoots and excited laughter. After everyone held a cup, she motioned to stop the music. "I'd like to make a toast." She raised her cup. "To friends — old and new. Happy hearts and easy minds."

Jane sniffed the cup and swallowed. The smooth burn of good bourbon heated her throat and warmed her stomach. She watched as Marcie quaffed her cup like a pro. It never ceased to surprise Jane that she absolutely could *not* tell a book by its cover.

Ramona smiled and said to Desiree, "Now I know why you moaned and groaned every time you buckled on that backpack."

"Or why I sounded like my shoes were full of water when I walked." Desiree laughed. "We've all worked hard getting up this mountain . . . I thought we deserved a treat." She raised her cup again and settled back on her blanket to applause and shouted appreciation.

Lu rose. "Moving right along . . ." she said lightly and turned to the others.

Marcie, apparently braced by the bourbon, stood, adjusted her bra decisively, and spoke with less hesitancy than Jane usually sensed in her. "This woman's spirituality thing is pretty new to me — but I think it's very beautiful. It's what I always hoped to find but didn't when I went on retreats with my church. Anyhow — I'm very happy to be a part of this circle tonight."

She glanced shyly around at the seated women, then continued. "I was raised in an orphanage. I was never quite able to speak up for myself and so I spent a lotta time on kitchen duty. My only friend the whole time I was growin' up was one of the cooks. A big, old black woman who sang while she worked. She taught me some songs she said white folks didn't usually get to hear. I know a lot of spiritual songs from my choir years, but I'd rather sing ya'all one of the songs Mama Dulcie taught me."

She cleared her throat, filled her lungs and crooned a low bluesy hum. She slapped her leg to start the beat, pushing her body forward and back in a rowing motion. Her voice rose as she sang out the words of a song never written, but passed from mouth to ear of black women since slavery days.

Jane watched entranced, as Marcie, in the flickering firelight, became a young slave woman, rowing an imaginary canoe back to freedom in her African homeland, searching through villages for her lost babies. Poppy picked up the beat on her drum and Ray softly played her violin, conjuring a tearful woman-throated lament from the strings.

Jane took note of each woman's face as she listened to the special magic coming from the earnest young missionary. Desiree's eyes were closed and her hands lay palm up in her lap as she rocked to the rhythm. Tears flowed down her cheeks and sparkled in the firelight. Jane looked quickly away when Lu quietly took Desiree's hand in hers and held it.

Marcie ended her song and stepped back in alarm

as the women all stood, clapped and shouted. Then they all vied to hug her at once. She beamed while they showered her with praise.

Lu took charge and brought order back to the circle of women. At last they were all seated except Ramona, who had disappeared into the shadows after Marcie's song. Ray stood, bowed low from the waist, nestled her violin under her chin and pulled the bow lightly across the strings.

Jane let out her breath in relaxed appreciation of the familiar sound of the violin. The fingers of her left hand played an imaginary cello on her right forearm as Ray's instrument laughed, cried and spoke in a moving, emotion-filled woman-voice, telling of the romance and passion of gypsy life in long-ago Hungary.

Across the circle from Jane, Ramona stepped into the wavering firelight. Her black hair swung loose around her shoulders as she moved. She pulled a shawl of colorful scarves across her back and down her bare arms as she twirled slowly to the quickening tempo of Ray's violin. Light reflected from the golden hoops in her ears and from metallic discs on a chain around her left ankle.

Jane saw that Ramona had attached to the waist of her hiking shorts more of the scarves that usually held her hair in a bun at her neck. They swirled around her hips and slid open past her muscled thighs as she danced, barefooted, around the outer edge of the circle.

Ramona placed her hands on her waist, tilted her head back — holding them all with her impression of pent-up passion about to be loosed to the gathering speed of Ray's bow. She threw her head forward and bent low. Her long hair swept the ground. Then, with abandon, she leaped into the dance as the music grew faster.

Jane's bearings shifted. Her uncomfortable awareness of being seated with a group of women watching another woman dance faded and she was aware only of Ramona's lithe body dancing for her.

And she knew it was for her.

Her stomach quivered. Her nipples drew lightly with pleasure. Warmed by the whiskey, she lost herself in Ramona's flashing eyes. She envied the dance of the moonlight on Ramona's long slender neck. Her fingers ached to follow the shimmering line of her shoulders. Jane's eyes hungrily took in the grace of Ramona's fingers as she raised her arms in supplication — beckoning the moon above Jane's shoulder to come dance with her. To be her lover. Jane's body responded hotly to Ramona's enchantment and overrode the feeble warnings her mind sent to try to break the spell.

The women shouted, stamped their feet and clapped their hands to the heated rhythm. All except Jane — who sat immobile, mesmerized by Ramona's beauty — by her open invitation — her promise of . . . of . . .

Sex. Ohmygod! What am I doing? I can't do this! Jane crossed her arms over her midsection and felt her heart thumping wildly beneath her ribcage.

The music stopped. Ramona flashed a smile round the circle, curtsied and wrapped herself in the blanket Lu held out to her. She sat across from Jane and looked at her from smoldering eyes that hid nothing. Nothing at all.

Lu spoke, her voice husky with emotion. "That was wonderful. Thank you, Ray — and thank you, Ramona. What a treat."

She waited as the women applauded the last performance of the evening. "Tomorrow morning we go on our survival hikes. Let's stand and hold hands and ask our Mother's blessing for that endeavor."

Jane stood woodenly. She barely felt her hands being taken. She could not stop staring at Ramona, who stood directly across the fire from her. The blanket had fallen from Ramona's creamy shoulders and her breasts heaved from the effort of her dance. Thrills of a kind Jane had never before experienced raced from behind her knees and intensified in her groin, causing her nipples to pucker with excitement.

A delicious, libidinous spark traveled directly from Ramona's eyes and settled in Jane's vagina, urging her clitoris into pulsating action.

Jane's insistent brain finally won a hearing. *I can't do this. Oh please. No. Not me. I just can't be a . . . be a . . . LESBIAN!*

The word echoed through every corner of her mind like summer thunder. Her stomach lurched. She freed her hands and stumbled away from the circle toward the trees and safety. Safety and solace and time to think.

As she walked swiftly through the trees, the night air cooled the dampness between her legs. The confounding discovery of her wet panties brought Jane's flight to a sudden stop. She stepped off the trail behind a huge pine and slid her hand inside her clothing. Her fingers slipped easily into the warm wetness. Tears of frustration, anger and longing flowed down her cheeks as she brought herself to furious orgasm, again and again — standing stiff-backed against the tree with the familiar face of the full moon as voyeur.

14

And Baby Makes Three

Although the high emotions of the solstice celebration still filled her, Desiree sat quietly as Lu performed her nightly ritual of meditating with her crystals and giving thanks to the Goddess. She gazed at Lu's strong silhouette in the light of a small candle as she finished her soft chant.

"Lucinda," Desiree said, "I love your face. Too bad we can't have babies. I bet they'd look just like you. Your face has all the character. My genes would just be a homogenizing influence. Maybe they'd have my eyes, though. God, they'd be great-looking kids. My green eyes and your red hair and that marvelous Blassingame nose of yours."

Lu turned to Desiree. "The last time you called me Lucinda was when you went Shirley MacLaine on me and got that wild hair to go mountain climbing in Nepal. And wanted me to take Sherpa guide training. If the Goddess has blessed me with any psychic sensitivity at all . . . I'd say we're getting close to abominable snowperson country again."

"Oh, honey," Desiree answered, with her eyes wide. "Am I that easy to figure?"

"After twelve years with you, darlin', don't you think I have a teeny head start on the poor civilians out there who don't know you?"

Desiree decided to take another tack. "That whiskey was good. Want another sip?" She held out a cup in Lu's direction.

Lu grinned in response, took a small taste and handed it back. "Now what's this all about, Des? You've been tap-dancing around the edge of something ever since we left Houston. What's going on with you?"

"Well, as far as I can tell, it started shortly after my thirty-second birthday."

"Wasn't that about the time you transferred to pediatrics?"

"Unh hunh," she nodded. "But that was OK. I didn't start getting these weird feelings until they put me on the infants' wing."

"Weird feelings?"

"Yeah. Every time I hold a baby and then have to put it down I get an awful feeling somewhere around here." She jerked her thumb toward her solar plexus. "And then I cry . . . every time. It's gotten to the point where I can't wear eye makeup on my lower lashes anymore."

Desiree felt tears well up, right on cue, in the corners of her eyes. She paid close attention to Lu, as Lu cocked an eyebrow and spoke.

"Maybe you're holding them wrong."

"It's not funny, Lu."

Lu held out her arms and Desiree snuggled close, trying not to sniffle as the tears flooded out. "Well, honey, you've got to admit, it's certainly out of character for you — the great number one Jane Fonda junkie — to admit motherly feelings. She of the body beautiful who would rather drink hemlock than suffer the stretch marks of maternity . . . I've always had a sneaking suspicion that attitude was at least partly responsible for your choice of lifestyle."

Desiree gathered her courage for a moment before speaking. "Lu?"

"Mmmm, honey . . ."

"Uh . . . Lu?"

"What, sweetheart?"

Desiree sat up and leaned back so she could see Lu's face.

"Can we have a baby?"

"You mean a *human* baby? Actually raise a child? Honey, you know it's next to impossible for lesbians to legally adopt."

"Well . . . there are other ways to get a baby."

"Des . . . I don't think . . . Are you suggesting we *buy* one?"

"No. I mean, I don't think I am. What I'm thinking of is artificial insemination."

85

"Whoa!" Lu blinked rapidly. "You're really serious, aren't you?"

Desiree nodded firmly. "See — I don't want somebody else's baby, Lu. I want *our* baby. With red hair and your nose."

"But, honey — that bourbon's got your thinking tangled. It wouldn't be *our* baby. It would be *your* baby. Yours and a red-head whomevers. It wouldn't look like me unless *I* had it."

Desiree nodded again. She watched Lu's jaw go slack as she understood the true intent of Desiree's suggestion.

"No . . . no, Desiree. I will not have a child so you can play mother. If you want a baby . . . I suggest *you* have one. I'll help you raise it. I'll even love it. But, *no, I won't have it for you!*"

"No" was not a word Desiree heard often. She stared at Lu.

Lu glared at Desiree. "I'm going to sleep now. Good night and good *luck!*"

She turned icily toward the tent wall. Desire stared at the lump Lu's rigid shoulders made under the sleeping bag. She sniffed, hooked a finger in the top of the whiskey jug and huffed out of the tent. She sat morosely by the dying fire and shivered under a damp towel left out to air.

15

What a Tangled Web . . .

The next morning Poppy was up early. She sat on a rock facing in the direction of the first faint light of the sun. She mentally ran down the list of equipment she would need when she took this last hike up to her secret place: the place where Irma had told her of the cancer that had taken her from Poppy in less than a year. That high, holy place with the big rocks that would be Poppy's funeral bier.

She had thought of little else in the past few

months, ever since the idea had caught fire in her brain. Dignity, she thought. To die at a time and place of her own choosing. Not like Irma — who had had to die in that ugly sterile hospital room away from all the things she loved. Soon Poppy would join her. Thirty-six years she'd had with Irma. Even now, four years after her death, memories of their life together stabbed Poppy's heart with more pain than she thought she could bear.

Kay scattered her thoughts by vigorously banging at a pan with a spoon. "Reveille!" she shouted. "Everyone up! This is the big day."

Muffled groans sounded from the scattering of tents. Signs of life showed as first Lu, then the others stretched, groaned and shivered out in the cool dawn air. Soon smells of breakfast mixed with the evergreen aroma of the mountain morning.

Poppy watched with detached interest as the women readied themselves for their twenty-four hour survival hike. Buddies were to go together. No food except emergency rations and water would be taken. The purpose of the hike was to give each woman the experience of living as close to nature as possible. With only a bedroll and a survival kit consisting of twine, fishhooks, matches, snakebite remedy and a knife, each team would find food, make a shelter and survive twenty-four hours in the woods without the comforts of civilization, and they would do it far away from the others with no lights and only a compass to guide them.

Marcie appeared at breakfast wrapped in her blanket, stooped and moaning. "I'm sorry, but I can't go, Jane." She looked extremely miserable. "I've got the cramps so bad I can hardly move."

Jane seemed disappointed and opened her mouth to answer but Poppy chimed in with, "Well, Ladybug — you're not the only one with problems. It's been years since I've had the monthly miseries — but my arthritis is on the prod. My joints feel like they're all fused together this morning. I don't think I'd better try sleeping in the cold woods tonight."

Jane again attempted to speak, but Poppy cut her off. "So that means Ramona can be your partner, Janey. No sense in you girls having to miss out on the hike."

Poppy could not keep from enjoying the look of consternation on Jane's face and the corresponding expression of joy in Ramona's eyes.

Kay stood, commanding their attention by rapping on the pan. "I guess that settles it then. Head 'em up and move 'em out," she said in her best "Rawhide" imitation.

Poppy noted with sadness that there seemed to be a cool tension between her old friends from Houston. Lu held herself erect and aloof while Desiree looked like an ad for Alka-Seltzer.

A sudden pall of regret descended on Poppy. The thought of leaving her friends cut her like a dull knife. She became aware of Marcie, who sat staring at her intently. She shrugged off a sense of alarm and set about tidying the belongings she would leave behind. She had written her will and goodbye letter long before the trek had begun.

She crawled into her tent to be alone with her thoughts until mid-morning when she planned to take her last hike up the mountain.

16

And Now I Lay Me . . .

Jane watched Lu and Desiree as they walked away, following the stream on its course downhill from the camp. Lu strode ahead with purpose but Desiree lagged behind. Jane thought Desiree had looked a bit peaked at breakfast. At least that part of her face not covered by sunglasses had appeared pale.

She turned her attention to the other members of their group who would remain in camp. Marcie still sat huddled by the fire in spite of Kay's best efforts to move her. Kay and Ray bustled about the camping area, busily constructing something with rocks by the firepit. Maybe a permanent barbecue pit for future hikers to use.

Poppy was not in sight.

Jane waited impatiently for Ramona to join her so they could leave. They had won the toss and the right to hike *up* the stream. Hard going up, but easy coming back down. It would be next to impossible to get lost if they kept to the little stream.

Ramona emerged from her tent and walked through camp toward her. She wore black jeans and hiking boots. Her white shirt blazed in the morning sun and her hair was caught back in a bun and held by a brilliant magenta scarf. She carried her pack and bedroll by the straps like a suitcase.

Jane had not looked directly at her since they had shared the intense moment across the fire last night after Ramona's dance. At breakfast she had avoided contact and now her knees trembled as her eyes drank in Ramona's beauty. Ramona stopped to say something to Marcie, then leaned forward to pat her shoulder. The action pulled her shirt tight across her back and outlined her long legs and the supple curves of her hips. Jane turned away as the tremble in her knees transferred like a shot to her groin.

No. I will not let this happen to me. This madness will pass. I will keep my mind on other things and it . . . will . . . pass. She knelt and tugged at the straps and buckles of her backpack and did not look up when Ramona spoke.

"I'm ready, Jane. Let's go. You lead and I'll follow."

Jane buckled on her gear and set a fast pace

91

upstream. Her long strides covered the ground with breakneck speed, as if she might outrun her problem. They scrambled over rocks, around deadfalls and through thick underbrush as they followed the course of the little stream upward toward its source for more than four hours. They trudged solemnly on, stopping only for a few minutes at a time.

The plan was to hike until the sun was straight overhead, then find food and make shelter for the coming night.

Jane spoke to Ramona only when absolutely necessary and then only in monosyllables. She noted that Ramona's long legs kept up with hers easily and that she did not once complain.

* * * * *

Poppy surveyed the neat arrangement she had made of the things she meant to leave behind. She nodded in agreement with her inner voice and carefully spread her bedroll over the letter and other things that would give her away if discovered too soon.

She checked her backpack to make sure she had everything she would need when she reached her destination. Finally satisfied, she gathered her equipment and crept out of the little tent into the glaring light of mid-morning.

Kay and Ray were arranging large flat stones around the area of the fire pit. Marcie was nowhere to be seen. In her tent, probably, wrapped in her blanket. That girl would never make it in the wilds of South America. Laid up by the *cramps,* for crying out loud. And of course, Poppy had seen Desiree and

Lu and Jane and Ramona all embark on their survival hikes early that morning.

So far so good.

She approached Kay who stood still for a moment, wiping perspiration from her face with a red bandana. "Kay, I'm going just a little ways upstream. I'm feeling better now and I think a short walk will do these old bones some good. Besides, I remember some small pools up yonder a bit that used to have some nice trout in 'em."

Kay smiled and nodded. "How long you plan to be gone?"

"Well — I'll be back before evening. But, I know how I am when I get to fishing. Time gets away from me. I'm sure I'll be out the rest of the day."

Kay nodded again and grinned at Poppy. "Okay — but, be careful. I don't think I'm gonna feel like hiking up this mountain looking for lost dykes after all this rock-hauling." She punched Poppy's shoulder playfully and turned back to her task.

Poppy hummphed inwardly but said nothing out loud. In her haste and her driving need to accomplish her objective of dying, she was only dimly aware of how her disappearance might affect the others on the trek.

She turned away from camp and walked steadily uphill. Never looking back. Only forward. Forward to the oblivion she craved.

* * * * *

Not too far downstream a miserable young woman followed Poppy, furtively skulking from tree to hidey-hole and on to the next tree. Marcie's mind was occupied with the conclusion she had reached about Poppy.

She had just decided to go and talk to the crusty old woman when she had heard Kay and Poppy talking, then watched helplessly as Poppy took off upstream. She grabbed her backpack and followed, careful not to let Poppy see her. The last thing she wanted was for Poppy to send her back to camp.

Besides, maybe if Poppy got to fishing it would be easier to sound her out. Maybe it was only Marcie's imagination. Maybe Poppy wasn't considering suicide at all. Sometimes older people were just hard to figure out. But all the signs were there. Just like they taught her in seminary.

* * * * *

Poppy stopped and rested occasionally, but not for long. Her need for peace nattered inside her head like a mother hen over chicks. Rustling . . . clucking . . . lulling her with a promise of warm protective darkness.

She spied a familiar landmark of jagged grey rocks. She adjusted her course away from the stream and followed a small trickle of water that rose from a spring about an hour's hard climb to the north. By checking her watch against landmarks she passed, Poppy realized that she had slowed over the years. An hour had lapsed since she veered away from the main stream and still she was only halfway to her destination. Simply carrying her walking stick became a chore. Her heart fluttered and her knees trembled with the effort of her climb, reinforcing her sense of having made the right decision. Yep. It was time to go.

The landscape changed abruptly from mostly green to mostly grey and black. A fire had burnt off much of the older growth of forest along her path. The bare, charred hulks of trees seemed fitting witness to Poppy's last hours. The fire must have happened in late spring, because very little underbrush had grown back.

She stopped, shaded her eyes, and drew a bead up between the tops of the blackened trees. There it was. Irma's Stonehenge. Rotted tips of vertical lava pegs pushed out of the earth in a ragged, gap-toothed oval. The tallest was nearly thirty feet high and the others graduated down to about as tall as a woman.

Poppy left the tiny stream and struck off in a direct line toward the megalithic lava formations, drawn by vivid memories of past campouts in the lee of their protective presence.

* * * * *

Marcie stopped and squatted behind a rock when Poppy stopped on the trail ahead. Her bladder demanded immediate relief. She finished her business as quickly as possible and peeked around the edge of the rock.

Poppy had disappeared. Marcie climbed rapidly up the trail, hurrying to catch up with the older woman. She was frantic to catch sight of her red socks or purple bandana flashing against the rocks up ahead. She congratulated herself for having had the presence of mind to tie a strip of her red neckerchief on a

limb pointing away from the main stream when
Poppy turned off its course to follow the smaller one.
She only hoped it wouldn't be necessary for anyone
to have to follow the way it pointed, or, for that
matter, any of the other markers she had tied along
the way.

17

Hook, Line and Sinker

Around two o'clock Ramona and Jane climbed a steep hill down which the stream they were following leaped and gurgled. They topped the rise and stood looking at a beautiful still pool that gathered in a glen where outcroppings of rock formed a series of v-shaped hollows. Tall pines growing along the near side of the narrow pool offered shade and shelter.

Jane shed her load of camping gear and sat on

the flat rock ledge. She filled her eyes with the pristine beauty and let her tired body relax.

"Oooohh," Ramona breathed as she sat on the rock beside her. "This is wonderful."

Her backpack joined Jane's with a *whump*. "Oh, look Jane . . . a fish! There's a fish down there." She pointed straight down into the pool at their feet.

Jane lay flat on the rock, shaded her eyes with one hand and peered into the clear water. Dark fish shapes hovered along the bottom with their heads pointed upstream. Her empty stomach identified them immediately as supper and she watched hungrily as they slowly undulated fin and tail in the barely moving water.

"You're wrong, kiddo." Jane said with a grin.

Ramona faced her, puzzled.

"There's *fishes* down there. *Lots* of fishes. Now — problem is — what do we catch 'em with?"

She surveyed their immediate surroundings for something to serve as bait while Ramona rummaged in her backpack.

Ramona cleared her throat.

"Uh . . . Jane?" She held out her fist. "Will this do?"

Jane yelped with delight as Ramona uncurled her slender fingers and exposed a handful of tangled fishhooks and feathers. "Trout flies! You're a genius."

Jane separated a colorful yellow and black beauty from the rest and tied it quickly to the end of the spool of line Ramona handed her. She motioned for Ramona to come with her and both women walked alongside the pool and stood just past the upstream end.

"How did you happen to bring trout flies with you?" She reeled off a few yards of line and tossed the fly as far out across the pool as she could.

"Kay's list said to bring something to catch fish with. I went to the sporting goods store and the clerk asked me where I was going fishing. I told her the Ozarks and she said I'd probably only find brook trout and these little fishhooks with feathers would be my best bet."

Jane grinned at her and played out more line as the slow current caught the fly and floated it toward the rock ledge where their orange backpacks lay. "Well — as a flat-land angler — I brought the usual corks and weights . . . I didn't think about . . . *Zoweee!* Look at *that!*"

The glen echoed with shouts and splashes as the surface of the pool erupted and sparkling droplets of water flew through the air. A large trout leaped high out of the water and almost pulled the line from Jane's surprised hands.

"Oh no you don't!" Jane shouted at the fish as she ran around the side of the pool going hand over hand down the line as she neared the rock ledge.

She thrust the line at Ramona who was right on her heels. "Here! Hang on to this." Ramona responded by wrapping it firmly around her hand.

The line zinged taut and scraped across the rock as the trout headed for deep water. Jane's stomach tightened at the possibility of losing their supper. She grasped the line, got a good purchase on it, stood and held it away from the jagged rock.

"Watch out!" She stepped back quickly — pulling hard as she did. The trout came out of the water with a *whoosh*. Jane, Ramona and the fish all rolled in a tangled heap away from the edge of the pool and came to rest against the exposed roots of a half-fallen tree.

The frantic trout flopped wildly beneath the bleached-out roots, firmly caught by the fouled line and the unyielding hook.

The women untangled themselves and tried to stand. They bumped heads and fell again, a replay of their initial encounter before the trek began. They looked at each other solemnly and both began to laugh at once.

Jane caught her breath finally and said, "Deja vu, Pocahontas?"

"Ooo-hoo-hoo," Ramona rubbed at her streaming eyes. "Yes — Jungle Jane — I do believe we've been here before."

They rose, giggling and weak, and rescued their prize fish from its prison. Similar fishing attempts netted two more average-sized trout. Excitement replaced Jane's earlier mood and her wit sparkled as they cleaned the fish and started a fire for cooking.

Ramona looked at Jane with a twinkle in her dark eyes. "I brought something else."

Jane looked sharply at the items Ramona offered, then smiled as Ramona produced a large sheet of aluminum foil and a plastic bag containing a grainy, dirty looking substance. She opened the bag and held it out to Jane. "Smell."

Jane leaned forward and sniffed. "Wow — fish seasoning. You think of everything!"

They wrapped the fish in the foil and put it on the coals to slow-bake while they rigged up a simple shelter by propping pine boughs against a great fallen tree near which they would sleep.

* * * * *

Poppy dropped her olive-drab backpack beside a half circle of rocks near the tallest of the lava cones. She lowered herself creakily to the ground, stretched out on her back and rested her head on her hands. A hawk floated in a lazy circle against the intense blue sky.

"Sorry, old woman," Poppy said to the hawk. "I'll only be in your hair for a little while."

Feathers, Dillworth . . . birds don't have hair. "Yeah. Feathers." Poppy answered her inner voice.

She rose and laid out the items she would need first. A length of strong nylon rope knotted at one foot-intervals attached to a three-pronged metal device, and another thirty-foot length of rope, one end of which she tied securely to the straps of her backpack. She worked quickly, humming bits of song as she looped the knotted rope like a lariat in loose folds around her left arm.

Poppy gazed intently at the top of the tallest lava peg. She walked back a little, then over a few steps. Happy with her position, she swung the metal device around and around, looping up into the air and back toward the ground in widening circles.

On the fourth swing she let it go in a *whoosh* as the rope played out. It sailed up and over the top lip of the rock. She pulled the rope taut and tested it with her weight to see if it had caught securely. It had.

She sat for a moment on a flat rock that had been placed on other similar rocks and surveyed the circle of grey lava-rock pillars and the remnants of the blackened forest beyond.

She looked back at the sky and the circling hawk. "Okay, old woman, get set. Here I come, ready or not."

Poppy tied the loose end of rope onto her belt, connecting herself to her backpack, yanked again on the knotted rope hanging down the side of the rock and begun to climb slowly, hand over hand. She fitted her toes surely into worn foot-holds chipped long ago into the side of the rock. She and Irma had discovered them on their first trip to the holy place twenty-two, no . . . twenty-three or . . . maybe twenty-four years ago.

Pay attention, you old fool. You're liable to fall off this rock and kill yourself!

She laughed out loud at the absurdity of accidentally dying from the effort of trying to kill herself and almost lost her hold on the next knot.

With one last puffing effort, Poppy hoisted herself over the edge and into the bowl-like indentation on the top. She first pulled up the knotted rope, then the one attached to her backpack. It bumped and scraped against the rock but was soon inside the sacred bowl with her. Memories of Irma crowded so close she thought she would lose her breath. She could see her now, hear her wild joyous squeals when she discovered the markings left by ancient Indians.

Poppy leaned back, cradled by the rock and her memories. She watched the hawk come lower and lower, but her eyes did not really see it. She was in another time. Her body rested from the unaccustomed exertion of the climb.

* * * * *

Marcie clambered through deadfalls, traversed areas of lush growth skipped over by the fire, scurried around and over increasingly rough rocky outcrops. She fought the panic that threatened to overtake her. She had not seen Poppy again. The flow of water in the tiny stream slowed to a trickle, then disappeared into a pool around the bottom of a huge boulder. She had come all the way to the spring and still no Poppy. She climbed the rocky cliff face and crawled out on the top of the rock covering the spring. She shaded her eyes and let her gaze travel slowly over the charred landscape, hoping for a flash of color.

Movement caught her eyes and she looked up quickly to see a large hawk gliding stiff-winged on an invisible current of air. Her gaze dropped from the hawk and fell on a cluster of grey stones poking up out of the blackened hillside, higher than the rock she was crouching on.

But, no Poppy. Nothing moved except the hawk. Marcie laid her head on her hands and silently sobbed her frustration and anxiety out onto the warm surface of the rock. The feelings of self reliance she craved had certainly not followed on the heels of independent action in *this* case.

Pum-pum-PUM-pumm . . . A drum sounded softly and a deep voice — unmistakably Poppy's — traveled up the hillside to Marcie's astonished ears. The sound seemed to come from the grouping of grey stones. Marcie bounced and slipped down the rocky ledge and set off on a nearly straight course for Poppy's voice.

* * * * *

Poppy ended her chant and sat as close to cross-legged as she could manage in the center of the lopsided lava bowl. She had placed items of great spiritual significance in front of her.

Ellie's dog-tags and Irma's worn gold ring lay on either side of a yellowed photograph that was propped against a bottle of pink capsules. It was a picture of her and Irma taken in 1949 by her old friend May Ellen Birch when they had visited May and Juno's farm just outside Poppy's hometown of Brush Arbor.

Poppy had changed clothes. She wore her riding pinks. The very same ones, she noted with pride, that she had worn the day she and Irma met. The crown of the black derby had suffered from being stuffed in the backpack and she had been unable to pull the worn black boots past her swollen ankles. She didn't fret, though. The pleasant thought occurred to her that she didn't have to worry about waking up stiff and sore in the morning.

Not ever again.

She felt the knotty veins that pushed against her socks and grinned. Oh, the joy of it . . . not to have to think about clotting factors or support hose or *any*thing. She was happy with her appearance and besides, Irma wouldn't mind a bit. The tan jodhpurs and scarlet jacket fit her much the same as they had forty years ago, except for a bit of extra seatroom in the pants now and the jacket seams pulled a little across her rounded shoulders. *Not a bad layin' out suit at all.* She smiled down at her red socks and black high-top Reeboks. Not boots — but, not bad.

She picked up the photograph and wiped the tears from her eyes. She opened the amber plastic prescription bottle and dumped all twenty capsules into her hand. With no hesitation she placed the first two in her mouth, unscrewed the lid from her canteen and raised it to her lips.

"Poppeeeee . . . where are you-oooo?"

Shit.

"eeee . . . *Ans*wer meee!"

"Ptui!"

Poppy looked disgustedly at the slick, wet capsules in her hand. Marcie's frantic calling sent chills down her neck. One second later, just *one second later* and there would've been one helluva problem for them both. How in the name of the Goddess had that idiot child managed to find her?

"Poppy! I know you're up there. I heard you spit. I'm comin' up."

Muffled scrapings sounded below.

"Go away!" *You little dimwit.* Poppy dumped the saliva covered capsules and the eighteen dry ones off her hand onto the rock.

"No. I'm comin' up there . . . Eeeeekk!"

Whump!

"Marcie?"

Nothing. *Jesusmaryandjoseph!* Poppy's inner voice reverted in panic to monotheism.

She crawled to the edge and looked over at the ground. No Marcie.

"Marcie . . . are you all right?"

Still nothing.

Poppy quickly dropped the knotted rope down the side, clambered over the edge and shinnied down it to the ground.

Groans came from her right. She turned to find Marcie crumpled against the base of the rock with her arm twisted at an alarming angle.

105

Well. You can just chalk up dying for now, you old dragon. You dodged the silver bullet this time.

"And caught the fresh cowpie," she said aloud.

Skree-eee-ee the hawk cried from her perch in a tree just outside the circle of rocks.

"Go ahead, old woman, laugh it up. It *is* kinda funny," Poppy answered.

She felt up and down Marcie's body for any more problems, finding none other than a most likely broken arm. She turned her and immobilized the arm, then half-carried, half-dragged Marcie over to the semi-circle of flat stone seats. Marcie moaned in pain and fluttered her eyelids.

Better get up there and salvage some of those pills, Poppy thought, before Marcie fully regained consciousness and screamed bloody murder from the pain.

Poppy was back on top of the rock before she really even knew it. She gathered her things, stuffed them in her backpack, crammed the capsules in her jacket pocket and lowered the backpack to the ground. She followed quickly — once more hand-over-hand on the rope down the rock face.

18

Friendly Persuasion

The sun had lowered to the treetops and the air had begun to cool by the time Jane and Ramona finished the shelter and sat by the fire to eat. Jane carefully unwrapped the foil cover and divided the steaming fish between them. Juice dripped into the glowing coals and sparked and hissed.

"I'm glad we found something to eat — and something so delicious, too!" Jane said as she picked bits of succulent trout from the spiny skeleton.

"Silly pride, I guess — but I really didn't want to have to break into the emergency package Kay gave us."

"Me too," Ramona responded. "Mmm-mmmm," she sighed, contentedly licking her fingers. She leaned back and looked up at the sky for a long moment.

Jane unconsciously ran her tongue over her lips as her eyes followed the graceful curve of Ramona's neck down her collar line to the rounded shadows beneath the first button. She looked quickly away as Ramona dropped her chin suddenly to speak.

"Of all the things we've talked about, Jane — I don't think you've told me about your life in Dallas. I mean, where you live and work. What's your life like?" Ramona's eyes glowed with friendly warmth and a tiny spark Jane couldn't identify, but it didn't seem threatening.

"I work with numbers all day," she responded, grateful for something to talk about that did not add to her growing awareness of how much she liked to look at the beautiful woman who sat across the fire from her.

"I don't really like my job — but, it's something I seem to do well. And since I've worked there for twenty-one years . . . it seems foolish to think about starting another career this late in life. I can retire as early as fifty if I want to. That's only six more years."

To keep her hands busy with something safe, Jane methodically pulled frayed white cotton fibers from a tiny hole in the knee of her denim pants as she talked. Ramona added small sticks to the fire and poked at the embers, listening intently as Jane continued, "Where do I live? Now that's something else I really don't like, either. We'd only had our house in a north Dallas suburb for four years when my husband and I separated. So . . . fair-minded monster that he was . . . I got the kids, the house, and the house payments. He got the Marines and a posthumous purple heart."

Jane laughed, wryly. "Seems like I've spent most of my life doing what had to be done. And that usually didn't, in any way, dovetail with what I wanted to do . . . which was just to be left alone and be paid for playing my cello." She looked at Ramona. "This is beginning to sound more and more like poor little me, isn't it?"

"No — not exactly," Ramona answered softly, her eyes downcast, toying with a long piece of wood that burst into sudden brilliant plumes of orange flame and set warm shadows dancing across her elegant cheekbones.

She looked up at Jane. "More like someone who always chooses duty over pleasure. A good wife and mother. Probably a dutiful daughter, too, right?"

Jane's knee peeked from the expanding hole in her jeans. She worried at it now with the fingers of both hands, tying the threads together — causing the edges to pull and pucker. She felt the sting of tears at the truth in Ramona's answer and turned away from the pledge of comfort in her dark eyes.

As Jane dusted ashes from her jeans and prepared to rise, Ramona quickly spoke again. "I was fortunate to find Harold so early in my life. He provided very well for us. Our — my house in San Antonio is a great pleasure for me."

Jane settled back against her backpack and watched how Ramona used her hands as she talked.

109

She would place a stick on the coals and turn it over and around until it began to issue vents of smoke. She kept agitating and teasing it, causing its internal temperature to rise until its destiny could no longer be denied and it burst into brilliant consuming flame.

Jane's gaze traveled slowly from Ramona's strong fingers up her forearm, past the rolled-back white shirt cuff, up and around her shoulder, and lingered in the shadowed dip where her neck and collar met. She became aware that Ramona had stopped talking. She forced her eyes up to meet Ramona's and felt the jolting impact in her lower abdomen.

"We must talk about it, Jane."

Ohgodno.

Jane did not ask what. Nor did she respond in any other way.

"We shared an extremely intense kiss. I kissed you and you kissed me back." Ramona tilted her head a little and looked questioningly at Jane.

They sat silently, like two chiefs at a powwow vying for advantage. The crackling of the fire between them was the only sound.

Finally Jane spoke.

"I've thought about what happened, Ramona. And damn little else. I think it was an unlikely, though fairly natural, outgrowth of the high emotional state we were both in after our dangerous experience in the river." Jane crossed her arms over her solar plexus and bit the inside of her lip to forestall the tremble that threatened to start there.

Ohgod — I want to bury my face in that soft place beneath your first shirt-button.

She said, "I don't think we should lend it any more of our energy." Her lips closed decisively over

110

the last word and she reeled inwardly at the opposing view of her unspoken desires.

Ramona looked at her and smiled sweetly. With only the slightest hesitation she said, "Oh . . . well then, can we just be friends? That'd make me very happy. I can forget about it if you can."

Jane tried to answer but her throat constricted and her voice came out gravelly. The pit of her stomach dropped and she dealt with her frustration and anxiety by jumping to her feet and tugging open the bedroll section of her backpack.

"Ah . . . okay," she got out. "That's okay with me." She turned her eyes to the sky as if she had just discovered the shadows were growing decidedly longer, darkening the forest around them.

"I think it's time we went to b- . . . sleep." She felt her face warm and she tried to hide it from Ramona while they opened out their sleeping bags and arranged them so their feet would be toward the dying fire and their heads protected by the big dead tree and the pine boughs. The back of Jane's neck tingled as the edge of Ramona's bedroll lapped over the edge of her own.

I can't let this happen . . . I have to think of my job — my grandson . . . my children. Wolfie would die! And mother! She would . . . she'd . . . well, I'm strong. I can whip this aberration. Her spirit churned like a Bach concerto as a lifetime of habit shored up her efforts and she once more chose duty over all else.

They took awkward turns relieving themselves in the woods and tidied up their dinner mess.

Jane crawled into her sleeping bag first. It felt like heaven. Her aching muscles relaxed as she

111

snuggled safe in bed, like a pursued fox run to ground. She thought she would not be able to sleep, but her tired body assisted her. She was soon deeply asleep, leaving Ramona sitting by the campfire to watch the sunset alone.

19

Marcie Scams the Wizard

Lu cupped her hands and shouted up at the camp. "Hellloooo . . . Kay! Ray! Hellooo." She sagged with relief as Kay's blonde head appeared above the stair leading down to the tiny falls. "C'mon, Des. Thank the Mother, they're there!"

"What're you guys doin' back so soon?" Kay asked, when they were near enough to hear. "Y'all scared of the dark? The sun's just now going down, no boogers even out yet."

"Hush, Kay," Lu said, spreading her hands in front of her and pushing at the air between them. "Something's up . . . at least I *think* there is. Is Poppy in camp?"

"Nope. She went upstream to go fishin' 'bout ten this morning. But, it's okay, Marcie's with her. When I went to pull Marcie out of her tent for lunch — I found a note that said she'd gone fishing with Poppy." Kay stopped talking as the look of worry increased on Lu's face. "What's up, Lu?"

Lu sat heavily on the rock bench Kay and Ray had built. "If Des hadn't distracted me so badly with this baby business, I would've picked up on it sooner."

Kay raised an eyebrow at Desiree, who sat quietly by Lu, not touching her.

"It came to me when Des and I stopped to eat lunch. Des was pulling out little goodies she'd put into my backpack the day before — tuna, water crackers —"

"Tsk-tsk," Kay interrupted, waggling a finger at Desiree.

"Anyway," Lu continued, "she found the bear claw necklace that Poppy gave me last night after our celebration. Poppy said she was heading in a new direction. That she wasn't going to look back any more and wouldn't need things that just stirred up painful memories anyhow. It hit me then —" She smacked the side of her head with her hand, "— that Poppy does not intend to ever leave this mountain. The chant she sang last night is part of a Native American leave-taking rite."

Kay stared at her as understanding dawned.

"Yeah, Kay — I think Poppy means to kill herself."

Kay leaped to her feet, galvanized into action. "We've still got at least an hour before dark . . . and it's only one night past full moon. There'll be plenty enough light for tracking. Ray, get the stuff."

Ray, who had joined the group in time to hear Lu's last statement, was already in motion. She pressed one of two heavy zippered leather pouches into Lu's hand. "It's loaded. Fire three shots if they come back. If we find 'em, we'll do the same."

Desiree crawled from Poppy's tent, pale and shaken, waving a sheet of paper. "Pops left a note, Lu. You were right."

* * * * *

Poppy looked down at Marcie who showed no signs of regaining consciousness. A large knot had swelled over her left eye. Even in the fading light Poppy could tell it was turning greenish-blue.

She peeled out of her red jacket, spread it beside Marcie's inert form and rolled her cautiously onto it. She changed into the clothes she had earlier shed and used her extra items of clothing and those found in Marcie's backpack to cover Marcie.

Fine . . . just fine kettle of smelly fish this is! Don't think that arm's broken after all. That's good. But, she oughta wake up now. Don't know how far she made it up there before she fell.

Poppy looked up at the rock. Maybe eight or ten

feet at most. But that was enough to cause a concussion. *Evidently. Wondercrone! She's out like a mackerel.*

Poppy straightened herself, jammed her hands into the pockets of her windbreaker and walked slowly around Marcie. Bit by bit she quelled the panic that threatened to overwhelm her.

This was no kind of peace.

No peace at all.

She had prepared herself so well for this final trip up the mountain. Thoughts beyond this day had previously dropped off into the yawning chasm of what had once been her future. Now it was suddenly necessary to deal with living again.

A fire. She had to make a fire. Keep Marcie warm. A fire so someone could find them. The full realization of her predicament, of the worry and pain she must have caused the rest of the women — who surely by now had found her note — the weight of it all came crashing in on her. Tears swelled from the wrinkled corners of her eyes and coursed freely down her cheeks.

She brushed at the tears with angry fists and looked around for something to burn. Nature's fire had beaten her to most of the deadwood but she located pockets here and there that held enough dry wood for her needs.

Marcie moaned occasionally and threw off some of the clothing. Poppy didn't get too far away. She hovered around her young friend like an anxious farmer awaiting a prize heifer's first birthing. Lightning blushed inside the cloudtops far off in the southern sky as night purpled around them.

Soon she had a bright fire burning hotly between

116

the rocks in a space she hoped could be seen by rescuers. She sat on her now empty backpack near Marcie and leaned against the rock seat. She ran her dry cracked fingers lightly over Marcie's forehead.

Marcie's eyelids fluttered. Then opened slowly, gradually widening. " 'Zat you, Poppy?" she mumbled groggily.

"Well — who the hell does it look like?" Poppy asked, gruffly masking her unbounded relief.

"I dunno. I can't see anything. Is it dark?" She put her hand up to her forehead and felt gingerly around the knot.

Poppy's relief quickly died as this new fear took shape. "Can't you see the fire over there? Look." She pointed toward the light of the briskly burning fire.

"No . . . can't see anything, Poppy. I'm *blind*!" She struggled to rise. Panic drew her full lips flat. "God's punishing me! I can't see." She clasped her hands in supplication. "I'm sorry, God. I know I shouldna had those thoughts about Desiree. I promise, God. If you'll just —"

Poppy got her arms around Marcie and held her close. "Oww — my arm!" Marcie complained.

"Shhh! . . . Hush. You're not blind. You're just temporarily unable to see. It's common to have a loss of vision after a fall like you took. Knocked your lights out, Ladybug. That's what you did."

Marcie quieted and Poppy felt her gradually relax against her.

"I do see little sparks, sort of. Like teeny flashbulbs. Maybe you're right. But how long do you think it'll be before I can see again?"

"Probably just a couple of hours or so," Poppy lied. "We'll just sit up here by the fire and keep

117

warm and pretty soon the others'll find us." She said, though she thought it unlikely the women would try to come after them until morning. Her stomach growled. Food had not been on her list of necessities when she had packed for this last hike.

Evidently having heard the rumble of Poppy's insides, Marcie said, "There's some stuff to eat in my backpack." Poppy hooked it with her walking stick and dragged it close. "In the little side pouch," Marcie directed.

Poppy eagerly rummaged for something solid among the layers of crumpled cellophane and gasped with delight at what appeared. "Peanut patties! Yum, yum." She rescued six of the pink sugared, peanut-filled little moons from the junkfood graveyard of Marcie's backpack.

They washed down the candy with shared swigs of water from Poppy's canteen. Irony tweaked her at the memory of the pink capsules she'd held in that same hand not long ago. She swiped at the tears that escaped down her face. *Crybaby — sentimental old fool. Stop this sniveling. What kinda crappy development is this anyway? All this boohooing. Folks'll think you've gone sappy.*

Marcie spoke, scattering her thoughts. "How come you're wearing that funny hat? It makes you look like a leprechaun."

Poppy jerked off the battered derby she had forgotten until now. "Well, I'll be damned," she said, turning it around in her hands like she'd never seen it before. "Hey!" she yelped. "Hey — you can see — you little shit! How long have you been . . . when did —"

118

"I don't know, Poppy. Just now, I guess. Don't get so excited. Besides, aren't you happy I'm not blind?"

"Of course I am. Ya damn betcha I am!" She hugged Marcie, forgetting about her arm.

"Ow, my arm hurts, Poppy," Marcie cautioned.

"Well, thank Goddess it's not broken." Christian monotheism disappeared now that panic's brief rule had ended. Poppy picked a grey and white hawk feather off the ground and stuck it in her hatband, then placed the hat on her head at a jaunty angle. "How come you followed me up here, youngun?" she asked as Marcie settled back against the rock, snuggling close to her side, beneath Poppy's protective arm. They sat watching the fire.

"I thought you meant to kill yourself, Poppy, and I didn't want to lose you. I know I'm not much, Poppy —" she continued over Poppy's protests. "But I really care about you. Maybe it comes from me being an orphan — I don't know. Or maybe it's that I feel like I love you like a daughter loves a mother. Anyway — all I know is I didn't want to lose out on knowing you for a long time to come. Besides I need somebody to teach me all the stuff a mother would, if I had one. I don't know *anything* about really *living,* Poppy."

Great. I'm a mother!

Well — that's not so bad . . . Is it? Well . . . is it? You wanted to die — poor baby — nobody wuvved ooo, did ums? So now somebody does. So deal with it, old dragon. Wake up and smell the coffee!

"Okay, *okay.*" Poppy startled Marcie by getting the last word with her inner dialogue by speaking

119

aloud. "Well," she said, softer. "I'm very touched, Marcie. I've never had children either — so I guess that makes me some kind of reverse orphan."

Marcie chuckled and, encouraged, Poppy continued,. "I've got a big old house in Dallas. Why don't you come to live with me and we'll see how this mom'n daughter stuff works out?" *Great Jehovah, where the hell did that idea come from? God-of-Panic tell us we didn't say that.*

She found it harder and harder to keep her mouth shut. Before she knew it she'd confided things to Marcie that she'd never told anyone except Irma. Like how difficult it was to swallow the bitter truth that she'd spent her whole adult life pounding a typewriter in the Caliche County Sheriff's Department. Forty-five years. A lifetime of wanting to be the Lone Ranger and having to settle for Senior Clerk. Not even a badge. Just a khaki uniform with a round patch on the shoulder and a white plastic nametag. And by the time they let the women wear slacks, the thing she was happiest about was that they covered up her support hose.

And where the hell was Women's Lib when she needed it? It came along too late for her. By the time women were allowed to wear guns she was too goddamn old to qualify!

She felt Marcie nod against her shoulder. *Great Goddess. Put the child to sleep, why don't you?* Old information about concussion victims swam to the top of her consciousness.

"Hey! Nope — can't go to sleep! Marcie." She shook Marcie's leg. "Wake up, Ladybug."

"Unnnnnnh," Marcie groaned. "I've got a terrible headache."

"I guess you do, hon," Poppy agreed. "But I can't give you anything for it. I'm afraid being knocked out is a pretty traumatic thing. Don't want to give your body anything else to struggle with . . . why don't you talk to me for a while? I'm thinking you should stay awake as long as possible."

"Okay . . . well . . . you know, Poppy, that stuff you said about being the Lone Ranger."

Thank you, Mouth.

"Well — when I was a kid I always wanted to be a detective. I read every whodunit I could get my hands on . . . Couldn't you start your own detective agency? I mean, I don't think there's any law that says you can't be a private eye . . . You listenin', Poppy?"

"Yeah . . . I'm listening." *If I'm not gonna die — I might as well be listening.*

"I'm beginning to think I might have a few pretty big problems in the way of my being a missionary. I mean I've been having some pretty odd thoughts lately . . . ya know?"

Poppy knew.

"And I think I could be a pretty good detective with the proper trainin'." Marcie grew silent.

"You? A detective? C'mon Marcie." Poppy chuckled.

"Well . . . I figured out what you were up to and followed you up here, didn't I?"

Poppy turned to face Marcie, shame-faced at her misjudgment of the younger woman's perspicacity.

"So you did, Marcie. At first I didn't think I was grateful . . . but I've changed my mind!" She grabbed Marcie to her and hugged her, careful this time of her arm. The girl would probably make a pretty good Tonto anyhow.

The old ticker must not be bad after all. Hadda been, woulda kicked out on me after all those trips up and down that rock. If I'm not dead from arthritis in the morning . . . guess I'll stick around for a while and see if the girl's idea is worth its salt.

She settled back with her arm still around Marcie's shoulder and grinned widely at the fire, then grinned even more widely as she realized that Marcie had shed the constricting bra that had eaten into her shoulders. She patted her young friend's neck in silent approval of this show of independence.

"Hey! You old letch! What the hell's going on here?" Kay's shout caused Poppy's heart to leap.

Ray added her two cents worth. "What's the funny hat for? Some kinda kinky party comin' down — I didn't get invited? Half the woods're burnt down up here. You women do that, Poppy?"

Poppy hugged Marcie tighter as relief flooded through her. "I'm glad we ate all the peanut patties. If we don't feed 'em, maybe they'll leave."

Marcie nodded and grinned at Poppy's stage whisper.

20

A Li'l Birdie

Desiree turned up the plastic jug with a slightly exaggerated flourish, and drained the last of the bourbon into a cup. She was celebrating the obvious meaning of the three distant shots they had just heard. She sipped a little and looked longingly at Lu, who faced away from her on the rock bench by the fire, busy with her evening rituals. She admired the way the firelight glinted from Lu's coppery hair.

Love that woman. Always have — always will.

Only human bean I ever did *love. Do anything for* her. *She could have just one little ole baby for* me. *Wouldn't hurt. Her pelvis is wider than mine. No problem.*

A sudden shrill peeping insinuated itself into her awareness. She peered into the dark underbrush trying to locate it. The raucous insistence of the sound pulled her to her feet. She put the cup down and walked unsteadily toward the trees, almost out of the glow cast by the fire.

Her frustration and curiosity grew as the peeping rose to a long frantic *cheeeeeeeeeeeeep*! She lurched backward out of the path of a very long, lumpy snake. Its mouth was full of feathers and it moved very clumsily for a snake.

Desiree assessed the situation immediately, even in her own slightly clumsy state, as one requiring violent intervention. She stooped, lifted a stone so heavy her arms trembled as she raised it over her head.

"Heeeyahhhh!"

Splat!

"Take *that,* you bird-gobblin *sonuvabitch*!"

Pent-up rage and frustration flowed from her in waves. She felt her hair lift and quiver, Medusa-like. All the anger and hurt in her had found a focal point for release and it drained out, dripping almost audibly onto the ground around her.

The snake, squarely pinned beneath the stone, writhed weakly for a moment and then lay motionless.

A rustling, flapping noise claimed Desiree's attention. She turned to see a flash of white as a mockingbird scrabbled along the ground dragging one white wing and hid trembling under the cover of a wide-leafed bush.

Desiree stood as still as the stone with which she had bombed the serpent. The reality of what had happened to the mother bird as it tried to distract and prevent the snake from eating her babies, and then the horror of being herself almost eaten after the babies were gone hit Desiree exactly where she lived.

She snarled as another bolt of rage gathered behind her flashing green eyes. She whirled, ran back and retrieved the cup of whiskey. She dragged the stone off the snake and soaked its bloody head and body with the bourbon. Then she dug frantically in the pocket of her tight shorts for a book of matches. In only four strikes the babyeater was in flames.

Desiree stooped, easily captured the mortally wounded mockingbird, walked a few wobbly paces away and sat on the ground watching the weak wisps of steam and smoke rise from the remains of the hapless snake.

"Honey." Lu appeared beside her. "What in the *world* are you doing?"

"I'm b-b-*barbecuing* that s-sonuvabitch!" Desiree stammered as the remnants of her anger leaked out, merging with her tears.

"Oh, Lu!" Desiree held the now limp body of the bird out toward her friend. "It's dead. I didn't save it after all."

She turned her tear-streaked face up to Lu. "I've been so selfish all my life. Me. *Me.* Everything always for *me.* The little I had left over I gave to you. All you've gotten for the last twelve years was just leftovers, honey. Leftover feelings — manufactured emotions. Day-old *stuff* from the world's greatest female impersonator! I'm sick and tired of being bitchy ole *me*! I wanna be a real woman. I wanna have a baby! *My* baby. Right here inside my body."

She poked at her lower abdomen, forgetting the bird in her distress. Her eyes widened as loosened feathers floated around her.

Desiree's face took on a determined set as she looked from the bird back to Lu, who now squatted in front of her. "Even if I end up like this, Lu . . ." She lifted the hand that held the bird. "I want to share myself with a child. I want to give the best of me to you and our baby, darling. Instead of keeping everything inside this made-up mask. The damn drag-show's over, Lu. From now on out I'm gonna be a real live woman if it kills me!"

She laughed tearily at her unintentional irony. "And that's another thing . . . I'm not gonna strangle my laugh any more. D'you know I haven't laughed right out loud since I was in puberty. Don't bray, Mother always said. It's so un-glamorous, dear. Bullshit! From here on in you're gonna think you're living with Santy-goddam-Claus! Ho, ho, ho!"

The sound echoed across the darkened valley. She smiled broadly at Lu, who clasped her in a fierce embrace. "I love you, crazy lady," Lu said and beamed at Desiree, who seemed to suddenly remember the bird.

"Let's bury this poor little critter."

"And cover up the snake-flambeau," Lu added.

"Oh yeah," Desiree answered, looking sheepishly at the charred reptile.

"Hon — I meant what I said. I really do want a baby."

126

"I know," Lu answered. "I do too. One with your green eyes and your homogenized genes."

Desiree started to stifle a giggle, then opened her mouth wide and laughed at Lu's pointed reply.

21

Ramona Takes a Chance

The twinkling bowl of the night sky had shifted significantly toward the horizon by the time Ramona stirred from her place by the campfire. She listened to the comforting, steady sound of Jane's breathing and the evocative calls of night-flying insects and small foraging animals in the forest around them. Far away to the south, tops of huge thunderheads glowed yellow and orange as lightning flashed through them. Nature had provided a fitting mirror for her inner turmoil.

She thought about the characters in the book Desiree had given her, Lane and Diana. Jane and Ramona. If only Jane would act on her desires in real life, as Lane had done in the book. Ramona *knew* Jane wanted her but was denying it. She had caught her looking more than once.

She held close the memory of Jane's blue eyes, of the way she looked at Ramona when she thought no one was watching. Her skin tingled at the recollection of Jane's pink tongue moistening her lips as her attention centered on the V where Ramona's breasts came together. She raised her hands to her breasts and felt the familiar weight of them in her palms. As her fingers brushed her hardened nipples, tiny shocks buzzed around her upper thighs and intensified into a warm pulsing between her legs.

Ramona was ecstatic and she was miserable. Her body yearned, nearly screamed, for the touch of the handsome woman who lay peacefully sleeping close by.

Friends. Ramona knew she could not be just friends with this woman. Their kiss by the waterfall had ended any possibility of mere friendship between them. After a lifetime of denial — of half-living — and then to have her body turned on like a Christmas tree by another woman's mouth . . . and *then* to be, once more, denied the fulfillment promised by those soft lips, strong arms . . .

Too much. Too damn much to ask. Damn her.

Damn her sky eyes! Damn her for sleeping while Ramona struggled alone to put out the fires Jane had started in the first place.

If we can't be friends then I probably won't have her at all. Because I can't be just friends. She'll go back to Dallas and I'll never see her again. Well then . . . what've I got to lose? I might as well send her back home with something to think about!

Ramona stood and slowly removed her clothing, with serene purpose, piece by piece, until she stood completely nude in the moonlight. She knelt beside Jane and slowly pulled the large zipper tab of her sleeping bag. *ZZZiippp . . . ziippp . . . zip!* Jane stirred and half-turned toward Ramona but did not wake.

ZZZiip — zip — zipipp.

"Jane . . . Janey . . ." She touched the sleeping woman's shoulder. "Jane — I'm scared and I'm cold." Which was true and not true. "Scoot over, Jane. I want to sleep with you." *True, ohgod, true.*

Jane mumbled grumpily and turned over, facing away, allowing Ramona room to slip in behind her. Ramona's heart drummed a triumphant rhythm as she settled into the quilted cocoon and prepared herself for metamorphosis. For the long-awaited freedom of flight. To soar on wings that had been folded for a lifetime.

She snuggled close to Jane and soaked up the warmth of her long body. Touching . . . at last . . . all the whole silky length of Jane's bare leg against her own.

Ramona trembled with anxious anticipation as she felt Jane's body stiffen and tense beside her. Jane gasped, just the tiniest puff of air, but Ramona knew

130

it for what it was. Jane was awake. Wide-eyed awake. And aware of Ramona's quivering presence against her back.

Ramona waited for Jane to decide what to do. Silent moments passed as she lay immobile, willing Jane with all the force of her being to make the next move. She finally felt an answering tremble in the woman-body next to hers as Jane's breathing shallowed and quickened. Ramona could stand it no longer. She turned on her side and pressed her naked length, spoon-fashion, against Jane's back and circled her free arm around her waist. She buried her nose and mouth in the soft hair at the nape of Jane's neck and felt her own hot breath flowing between them.

Jane moaned.

Ramona found the waistband of Jane's sweatshirt and gently slid her hand inside and up to rest against the velvety softness of Jane's stomach. She pressed lightly and moved her fingers in tiny circles.

"Ohh . . . God," Jane said softly. She grabbed Ramona's hand and held her fingers tightly, stopping their slow march up her ribcage. She turned over to face Ramona who breathlessly welcomed the tentative touch of Jane's fingers on her breasts, moving cautiously, questioning — as if to ascertain they really were naked.

Jane's tears splashed hot, then cool on Ramona's chest as the night air claimed them. She thrilled as Jane threw back the top of the sleeping bag, leaned over her and looked down at her hands, her eyes following the path of her fingers over and around Ramona's breasts. She lowered her weight slowly against Ramona.

Ramona slid her arms around Jane's shoulders and lightly held the back of her head. Her clitoris pulsed in response to the touch of Jane's lips against the sensitive skin of the large, high-mounded aureole surrounding her nipple. She arched upward, savoring the lovely weight of Jane's body covering hers as Jane explored and caressed a nipple with her tongue.

Jane moaned against Ramona's breast, moving quicker and breathing harder. Suddenly she stopped, trembled, pulled away and stood abruptly. Tears glistened on her face.

She stared down at Ramona, then looked up at the moon and shrugged with her hands turned palms up — passing some kind of private communication. She slowly crossed her arms and pulled her sweatshirt up from the bottom, past her head and peeled it off her arms. She hooked her thumbs in the waist of her panties, pushed them down to her knees and stepped gracefully from them to stand naked in the moon's light.

Ramona caught her breath at Jane's pale loveliness in the semidarkness. The kiss of moonglow across her strong shoulders revealed every curve and hollow for her to look upon.

Jane knelt and stretched out beside her. "I really can't stop myself, you know," she said, as she bent her head to Ramona's, their lips only a hair's breadth apart.

"I know," Ramona said quickly and the next thing Jane might have said, she didn't, because Ramona leaned forward and closed the gap between their lips. A current of fiery feeling flowed through her. A powerful quickening of every vein and sensor.

She gave herself completely to the thrilling excitement of knowing the lips moving against hers were Jane's. She felt no fear of the strong fingers now exploring, caressing her abdomen, her waist, down her hips and *God — ohgod yes* over her upper thighs. She parted her legs to create a natural terminus for Jane's hand.

Jane moaned a low crooning sound and the urgency of her kiss increased. Ramona moved, arching slowly upward to meet those woman fingers. Up and back and up again.

Touch me — ohgod — touch me there.

Jane covered Ramona's arching hips with the warmth and weight of her knee and moved her body against Ramona's, adapting to the rhythm of her thrusts.

I'm going to die from this. Ramona recognized the heat and fuzzy dampness of Jane's vulva against her hip. Desire exploded — unchecked, a chain of erupting tremors rocked her own center beneath Jane's knee.

She pulled back from their kiss. Her voice was low, throaty and urgent.

"I've never . . . felt like this . . . oh Jane. I must have more . . . Please . . . touch me down there with your fingers."

She saw with pleasure the whiteness of Jane's answering smile. Cool air rushed across her warm skin as Jane slid her knee downward, uncovering that dark throbbing place where all Ramona's feeling centered.

The light, inquisitive touch of Jane's fingers caused a gathering current of thrills to race outward to Ramona's arms, legs, hands, feet, torso, head. Brilliant light shapes played across the insides of her eyelids.

Ramona was barely conscious of the growing agitation and urgency of movement in the woman beside her. Nothing in the universe mattered except the fingers moving in and out, sliding past — lingering tantalizing against that greedy spot that cried for more.

Ohgod — More! Faster! Harder! Don't stop! Oh Jane ohgod — god . . .

"Ohh — oh Jane," Ramona whispered as consciousness rushed in on her.

Jane stiffened and shuddered beside her. She rubbed her wetness against Ramona's hip in a slow ecstatic grind. Then she raised herself over Ramona and sat lightly — straddling her, moving slowly, with obvious intent. She leaned forward and rested her upper body on her hands. The lovely surging weight of her breasts slid over Ramona's as she moved, up and back. She buried her mouth in Ramona's neck on every forward movement.

Ramona was astonished by the intensity of the emotion and physical pleasure that gripped her as Jane leaned back and increased the tempo of her thrusts. Her creamy breasts swayed in the moonlight as she threw her head back — ground her open vagina against the still pulsing, fleshy mound of Ramona's vulva. Ramona moved under her, trying to keep time with Jane's urgent need.

Suddenly Jane arched backward, and her rigid body shuddered as she keened a high moaning sigh. Then she lowered her upper body over Ramona's and relaxed against her.

Ramona held her close while Jane silently cried.

Jane's breathing slowly steadied and she sniffed against Ramona's collarbone. "I don't know why I'm crying." She sniffed again.

"It's okay."

"But it —"

"Shhhh. Let's just hold each other and sleep now," Ramona said, as Jane moved up and away from her, then settled against her side, warm now, away from the cooling night air, under the comforting cover of the quilted bag.

They snuggled close and for the first time in her memory, Ramona drifted into sleep without moving away into a detached, untouched space of her own that no one — ever — until now, had entered. She felt her whole being expand and sing an invitation to the woman who breathed into her hair. She floated closer to sleep, dimly aware of the inner rustling of unfolding wings. Jane's hand found hers, and she slept.

22

The Cold Light of Day

Fully dressed, watching the sunrise, Jane sat on Ramona's neatly folded sleeping bag by the rekindled fire. Ramona still slept in Jane's sleeping bag.

Jane wiped again at the tears that flowed, ebbed, then flowed again as she wrestled inwardly with the possible effect of last night's cataclysmic events on her life. She had indulged herself with complete unthinking abandon. The memory of her rush of orgasmic relief astride Ramona's achingly beautiful

136

body gathered in her vagina, throbbing, hardening her clitoris in hurtful need. She pinched her nipples, angrily, punishing them between her strong thumbs and forefingers.

No. I can never do that again! I will keep my mind busy with other things. I will not think about what I let myself do last night. I have too much at stake to let this happen to me.

Ramona stirred behind her, yawning and stretching.

"Jane. Are you making breakfast? I'm starved." She spoke playfully.

Jane turned to look at her. Black hair tumbled around creamy naked shoulders. Desire. Pain. Frustration. Anger. Need. *Ohjesus get hold of yourself. Straighten-up-JaneMaryJackson — this is your life dammit!*

She cleared her throat.

"Um, no. Ramona." *Don't stumble — do this right.* "I've been up for some time . . . thinking . . ." *Go on fool don't stop now.* ". . . about what happened last night. I owe you an apology," she finished in a rush.

Ramona's facial muscles slackened for a split second, like the sagging frosting on a cake at a Fourth of July picnic. Then Jane watched with admiration as she squared her shoulders and won the war against surprise.

"An apology?" she asked evenly, pulling the quilted sleeping bag a little tighter around her. "Did you do something wrong?" Her large brown eyes glowed amber in the morning light. The accusation in them pierced Jane's heart.

"Yes, Ramona. I did. It was weak and very wrong

137

of me to give in to a . . . p-purely physical need like I did."

Ramona smiled slowly and shook her head.

Can you die from being smiled at? R.I.P. — J.M.J. — killed by a smile.

"As I recall, Jane, I was the one who crawled into your sleeping bag with no clothes on . . . if there's an apology due — I suppose it should be me saying I'm sorry. But I won't say it, because I'm not sorry. I took a chance for happiness and I'll never be sorry for that. I experienced something priceless last night. I know now what I've been missing my whole life. You gave that to me and I'm grateful. If that's all I'm to have from you . . . then it'll have to be enough. I promise not to seduce you again."

Jane hung her head and looked at the ground. "You didn't do anything I hadn't already wished for. It was my fault, too. I must've given you some indication your advances would be welcomed." *Stuffy, Jane — why don't you just quit while you can?*

"I have just one last thing to say on the subject, and then I'll never mention it again. It'll be our secret." Ramona gazed at the woman who had given her so much pleasure.

Jane looked up into eyes that did not lie. Earth-eyes, truth-telling eyes.

"I want you, Jane — with all my heart. But the next move is up to you. Remember that. I'll be waiting."

She rose, dropped the sleeping bag from her naked body in a fluid graceful motion and walked calmly away from Jane toward the trees. It was a scene that was to replay itself in slow motion across Jane's

138

inner eye over and over again. And always with the same hot, wet result.

Jane closed her eyes against the sight of Ramona's sensuous walk and wrenched her thoughts away. She tapped the calloused outside of her left thumb against her teeth. She worried at the tiny ridges of loose hardened skin with her tongue. When she resumed her cello practice, the callouses would rebuild. She escaped inward, concentrating once more on the intricate fingering of that troublesome glissando, while Ramona dressed and prepared for their return to camp.

23

Back to the Future

The hike back down the stream to camp had been a painful blur for Ramona. Jane was intent on keeping to herself and had only spoken when absolutely necessary.

The other women were all excited and talked of little else but Marcie's heroism and Poppy's bumbling escapade, and of their individual plans for new projects when they got back to the lives they had left behind less than two weeks ago. For Ramona, the final days and nights swam together as the women made their way back down to the river and then to the jeeps.

Tonight would be the last night on the trail. Their last chance to celebrate the joys of nature, the freedom of roughing it. A festive atmosphere prevailed — except inside Ramona's heart, where nothing joyful lived.

Desiree had been a true lifesaver, understanding, lending support and comfort. But every time Jane forced a laugh or spoke within her hearing, Ramona battled a fierce blanketing despair. She longed for the peace of her home in San Antonio. Her piano, the cool white adobe walls, the comfort of familiar, loved surroundings. She had enough photographs for a new series of watercolors. She yearned to get home. Even Scrapper, Harold's cantankerous old cat, would seem easier to live with. Maybe two weeks at the kennel had imbued her with a little humility.

"Come'n git it." Kay banged her battered pan.

Ramona forced herself to line up, bowl in hand, for her portion of supper from the pot on the fire. The women jostled good naturedly as they waited for Kay to ladle out the steaming chili.

"Better hurry up — looks like a bit of weather's on the way," Kay warned, looking skyward.

A few moments later the cool downdraft of a quickly gathering summer storm swept over them, swirling leaves and grit. They had barely finished eating and were busily stowing away camping gear and cooking utensils when huge drops of rain splatted on the ground, kicking up little puffs of dust.

Ramona crawled into the tent with Poppy right on her heels. Squeals and cursing erupted behind them as the other women also made for shelter.

The rain drummed against the fabric of the tent until the sides sloped inward under its weight. Ramona was grateful for Ray's insistent teaching, checking and rechecking of proper tenting methods. Of course, Poppy was an old hand at roughing it, but she had insisted Ramona learn how to select a site and erect the tent.

Ramona peeked out the tiny, netting-covered window under the flap. The rain fell so hard she could barely make out the orange and blue tents across the firepit. Lightning flashed, leeching the color from the scene, and thunder boomed and crashed around them.

Poppy startled her by speaking close to her ear. "Well. I guess we've been pretty lucky, all told."

Ramona moved over so Poppy could look out the little window.

"Yep," Poppy continued, as she took her turn at the peephole. "Mother Nature's been real accommodating up until now. I reckon this takes care of anyone's plans for a big campfire tonight." She drew away and sat back on her bedroll.

Ramona didn't answer, but she wasn't disappointed. Just looking at Jane caused a heavy, enervating ache deep within her. She desperately wanted to get back home and try to pick up the threads of her life.

Poppy talked of her plans to start a detective agency as soon as she returned to Dallas, but she also tried to help Ramona understand Jane's behavior. With little success. What really made it so difficult was the sure knowledge that Jane was hurting too. That she battled fiercely against their attraction, but would not give in to it. No matter what.

Ramona finally slept, uncomfortable and shivering against the cold dampness that found its way inside her shelter.

* * * * *

Morning arrived, grey and dull with thick drizzly fog that rose from the river valley. Kay handed out granola bars along with her apologies. The group broke camp and slogged silently along the trail, each woman careful to keep up, the visibility so poor it would have been easy to become separated from the others. Intent on reaching the RV Park where the Jeeps were parked and getting at least a little warmer and dryer, they made good time despite the weather.

The sun struggled to shine but a heavy bank of thick dark grey clouds lowered over the valley, and the irritating drizzle became a steady light rain. Ramona's feet were soaked and she was thoroughly miserable.

"Yahoo!" Desiree let out a whoop as Kay and Ray's two red and black Cherokees and Jane's blue Toyota truck finally appeared before them.

Tears sprang to Ramona's eyes as she watched Jane unlock the rear window of the truck topper and efficiently stow her camping gear inside. She knew it was impossible, could never happen, but nonetheless she wished with all her heart that she were traveling with Jane to Denver where Jane was going to visit with her daughter, Isadora.

Ramona and Marcie had met the others at the

airport in St. Louis before the trek began, but since so many happy connections had been formed within the group, and everyone lived in Texas, they gladly accepted Kay's offer of a ride back home.

Ramona had invited Lu and Desiree to come visit with her for a few days in San Antonio and Marcie was stopping off in Dallas to visit with Poppy for a while.

Ramona was deeply pleased at the changes in Marcie and in Poppy. Marcie bloomed with a radiant new self-confidence and Poppy had miraculously begun to express hope and expectations for a productive future.

The constant dreary rain hurried them through what would otherwise have been lengthy goodbyes. Ramona was so distraught by the knowledge that she would probably never see Jane again that she paid scant attention to what was said to her. Her gaze kept coming to rest on Jane's tall resolute figure as she prepared for her trip to Colorado.

A rush of pain and longing filled Ramona when Jane stopped her frenetic activity and leaned her forehead against the roof of the truck topper. Her shoulders drooped and she crossed her arms across her middle, hugging herself. Then she turned slowly and her anguished blue eyes met Ramona's with an intensity that shook Ramona to the center of her being.

I will die from this. Oh Jane, I can't live without you. Don't leave — don't do this!

She felt her knees begin to give way as Jane walked toward her. Somehow she managed not to disgrace herself as Jane stopped in front of her and spoke softly. "I guess this is it, Pocahontas." She

144

held out her hand toward Ramona for the traditional handshake.

Ramona forced her mouth to smile as she held out an object she had been saving to give Jane when she got the chance.

Jane turned her hand up to receive it. Ramona knew she had scored a grand-slam as Jane's lower lip quivered and she closed her fingers around the black-and yellow-feathered trout fly.

"And no, Jungle Jane. This is not quite it." Ramona calmly broke her promise and made what was definitely a move. She shocked Jane and the other women by throwing her long arms around Jane, pinning her arms to her side. She kissed her full on the mouth, slow and hard, then turned and walked away, leaving Jane standing alone in the mud — blushing a ruddy, glowing red.

24

Not the Waltons

Three days later, after a brief but happy visit with her daughter in Denver, Jane headed the little blue truck out of Forth Worth toward the annual family reunion at her home town of Scatterbone about sixty miles northeast of Dallas. The truck was loaded with all the baby accoutrements that Wolfie and Rina couldn't get into their tiny hatchback: a playpen, walker, swing, highchair.

Her cargo brought back memories of her own

child-rearing years. The truck she now drove was a habit left over from Wolfie's teenage motorcycle phase. She'd bought the first truck then and found it so handy that it had become a fixture in her active, family-filled life.

The dry precision of Bach filled the air-conditioned cab with a metallic fury. *Pock-bockety-bock-pock,* like a jeweler's hammer, cool and geometric. Something in which she could invest her whole mind and spirit with no fear of physicality.

Even inside the truck, with blasts of frigid air blowing from the air-conditioner vents, trickles of perspiration crept from under her hair and down her neck as she drove through the blistering 2:00 p.m. heat of Independence Day. A classic Texas heat wave had kept the temperature over one hundred degrees for the past six days. Shimmering waves of heated air rose from the wide straight highway, fuzzing the horizon into layers of green and grey dryer lint. Garish, leaning fireworks stands cluttered the near landscape at every small town or intersecting roadway. Cattle in the fields crowded into the shade of any tree they could find and stood motionless, producing as little heat as possible. Only their tails moved as they brushed away the maddening ever-present heelflies.

Jane's mind slipped away from the controlling music back to her short visit with Isadora and their unsettling conversation just before Jane had left for Texas.

"Mom . . . don't you know why I moved way up here, away from the family?"

Jane had been hurt and puzzled at Isadora's insistence on attending college out of state. There had been an exchange of harsh words, especially after graduation, when she had expected her daughter to come back home and get a job close to the family who loved her and missed her.

"But, Izz, honey," Jane had countered. "Everyone'll be at the family reunion this year . . . everyone except you. You'll be the only grandchild not there."

"Fine. It'll give them something to talk about besides Aunt Carol's latest diet. They suffocate me with their concern about my affairs. I'm a grown woman, Mom. Hasn't it ever occurred to you that you are too? I bet you don't want to be there any more than I do. When you called and told me about that wilderness trek you were going on, I thought maybe you'd begun to see the light, but I guess I was wrong."

Blinded by the light! Oh, Ramona. What have I done?

"I'm sorry for your sake, Mom, because I know Granny'll blame you for my not being there. But I've got this chance to hike up along the Divide with Lawrence and I'm going."

The old familiar ache of guilt jolted Jane back to the unpleasant task she faced upon arrival at the family farm. She knew her mother would be difficult about Izzie's absence and the rapid-fire questions would begin.

The Bach tape ended and the moment sang with the sound of the tires on the road beneath and the whooshing hum of the air-conditioner. A new tape clicked in and the passionate, gypsy-like strains of Rimsky-Korsakov's *Capriccio Espagnol* swelled around and through Jane, igniting a flaming jet of

148

unexpected physical wanting. Her knees trembled and her clitoris hardened into urgent readiness as her psyche sought the excitement it craved. She relived flashes of Ramona.

Dark eyes, smoking at her across the campfire after her dance. Sinuous shape of her willing body arching up to meet the naked needy center of Jane's spread legs. Heavy breasts — hard-nippled in the cold morning air — soft gleaming mound of stomach above dark triangle — long legs walking away. Last hard kiss standing in the mud, captured by strong arms.

Ohgod — ohgod — I can't live this way.

Her strong left hand found the waistband of her cotton shorts. With breathless urgency she thrust her long fingers inside her clothing and into the wetness between her legs. The fiery music curled inside her chest and danced down her spine to merge with the raw feeling of flesh on flesh.

The truck slowed only a little as her foot eased on the accelerator. Quickly — efficiently — Jane stroked her need into climax as tears joined the convergence of perspiration that dampened the collar of her blouse.

As the spasms slowed and release flooded her body, Jane's brain seethed with an inexplicable cold fury. She slammed the heel of her hand against the stop button of the tape player, causing it to malfunction. Frustrated, she probed under the plastic flap for the tape, extracted it by force and flung it to the floorboard. Filmy spirals of brown tape curled out of the dash. She yanked it viciously, slicing her finger as the tape broke free.

She tromped on the gas pedal and sped through the holiday traffic with little concern for speedtraps.

149

Gravel scattered and dust spewed in clouds as she fishtailed off the pavement onto the country lane that led to her childhood home.

Great — just great. Home at last . . . about to be reunited with loving family. I smell like a rutting goat and I'm bleeding! Horseshit! Damn — damn — damn!

Jane sucked her wounded finger and stiffened her spine as the wide dark spaces and white railings of the many-porched farmhouse came into view. The deep green rows of "the family pines" stood guard over a colorful collection of cars, trucks, vans, and RVs.

The family pines. As a child Jane had taken great pride in her mother's unique tradition of planting and christening a new tree when a child was born into the family, but the tradition — begun by Jane's maternal great-grandmother — had become an obsession for Mavis, Jane's mother. She tended them with a fierce devotion that Jane and her sisters discussed regularly during their weekly phone calls. Mavis Porter Billingsly was a woman of strong principles. A widow of twenty-six years, she'd never considered remarrying. As far as Mavis was concerned, there was only one reason for bringing outsiders into the family . . . and she'd already produced children. She ruled her tiny matriarchy fairly — by the book. Her book.

The fourteen tallest pines grew in rows of six (Greatgrandma Mary Louisa had had six children) on each side of the wide driveway, and one each centered on either side of the front walk in the two equal squares of lawn. The lawn trees were Colonel Zebulon Porter and his wife Mary Louisa Porter. Even the toddlers knew that. The rest of the family trees marched away from the old house in succeedingly younger, shorter rows, until the newest stood at straggly attention, barely able to carry their copper name plates.

Jane couldn't help it. As always, her eye went to the left of the drive to her tree, fourth row out, first in line. As the eldest of three sisters, she grew closest to the house in the place of honor. Of course, the rows of mirror trees grew on the right side of the house, but everyone knew they were there only for aesthetic balance. The real trees were named and christened.

Jane unwound her long body from the truck cab and slid her fingers under her collar. The heat hit her skin like a belly flop into shallow water.

"Yo, Sissy! Over here!" John J., her sister Carol Lou's skinny husband, shouted at her from the recesses of the side porch. He stood in the shadows and thrust a hand holding a sweating can out into the sunlight. "C'mon up here and get a cold 'un."

She didn't bygod mind if she did. She mounted the steps, tightened her stomach and squared her shoulders against the loud huggy hellos that greeted her.

* * * * *

Dinner was chaotic as men and women, boys and girls of all ages jostled and vied for position in the line that passed by the loaded tables. Laughter, shouts and the go-together picnic odors of food and insect repellant filled the air. The holiday-crazed little ones kept the doors banging, and the overworked air conditioners waged a losing battle to cool the huge dining room.

Jane mopped her face with a wadded paper napkin and shifted her wriggling grandbaby to the other knee. She watched her daughter-in-law push bits of food around on her plate. "Rina, honey — you've been awful quiet. Got something on your mind?"

Rina shot a telling glance at Wolfie as she raised her head to answer Jane, but he was suddenly engrossed in scooping the seeds from a fresh jalapeño pepper. "I think the heat's got me down, Mama-Sis. Thanks for holding Sky so I could eat." She reached for the baby and walked away toward an air-conditioner, fanning the fussy child with a clean paper plate.

Jane's attention shifted quickly to the kitchen doorway where her mother stood on a chair, clamorously ringing a cowbell with one hand while holding aloft a camera in the other.

The crush of miserable overfed people moved out onto the lawn to gather in a well-rehearsed, regimented formation in front of the tallest pines. Jane's other brother-in-law, Smokey, married to her youngest sister, Portia, set up the tripod in the driveway. Mavis sat in her wicker chair, matriarchal middle of the clan. Propped against the chair leg was a placard proclaiming the date in big black numbers.

Smokey set the timer and dashed back to slip into his place beside Portia, who stood to Jane's left. Jane, directly behind her mother's chair, towered over it. Carol Lou, on her right, slipped an arm through hers — Portia did the same on the other side. Jane gripped the woven top of the chair with both hands and fixed her gaze wistfully on her mirror tree.

Everyone held position, like well-trained setters at point, while Smokey executed the backup shot.

Squirming children escaped the clutches of parents and sullen older siblings and dashed frenetically in and out of the trees. The tight row of people loosened and flowed slowly across the lawn, up the steps, onto the porches. It was time for the women to make home-made ice cream. The men gravitated to the task of fireworks management. Older teenagers alternately pouted or preened and sneaked around the outbuildings, downwind from the house, to smoke dope, tell jokes and try not to seem excited about the evening fireworks. A go-cart whined around a dusty circle as Portia's youngest son demonstrated his apparent going-straight-and-wildly-to-hell streak by maneuvering the go-cart in erratic, skidding patterns closer and annoyingly closer to the yard and sideporch, where the more duty-bound and therefore beloved grandchildren applied their varying strengths to the handles of recalcitrant ice-cream freezers.

Jane escaped the hubbub and walked across the lawns to the unimportant no-name trees. Walking in the shade of the pines forcibly brought back the memory of Ramona and their fishing adventure. *Ohgod — her laugh — those eyes. Us. Together. The feeling. I hurt. This will kill me.*

She sought out the tree that mirrored her own. Dropping to the grass, she leaned against the tree and looked away from the house at the two trees in the next row. The mirror trees for the ones planted when Wolfgang and Isadora were born. The slanting rays of the evening sun glinted on something nestled in the notch of the lowest limb on Isadora's tree.

Curious, Jane investigated. A small square mirror

framed in brown plastic was wedged into the bark. It had obviously been there for years. Jane worked it loose and rubbed it on the grass to clean it. She turned it over in the light. Something was written on the back. She wet her fingers and rubbed it, holding it so the sun caught the words scratched into it.

Look on the other side and see
The face of one who thinks like me
That people don't have roots like trees
                                   I.M.J.

She turned it over and studied her reflected face. She watched a tear slide past the corner of her nose and closed her eyes. *Izzie, Izzie. Dear child. You've always been so strong. Oh — what am I going to do?*

A shrill sound broke in upon her thoughts. Someone screaming. She jammed the mirror in her back pocket and sped through the trees and across the yard toward the commotion.

Mavis Billingsly was prostrate on the ground. Her arms formed a protective circle around the newest family tree. Or, at least, around what remained of it. Sky Walker Jackson's tree was mangled and shredded. A split and broken goner.

Carol Lou and Portia both looked meaningfully at Jane, who stopped in her tracks. Eyes widened and eyebrows arched as Sister shirked her duty to console Mother. Jane's younger sisters seized their moment and triumphantly gathered their near-hysterical mother from the ground so the sorting out and blaming could begin.

The go-cart lay upside down, wheels still slowly

spinning. Blame was quickly fixed on Portia's errant, red-eyed scion, who was loudly banished to the confines of the RV.

Attention centered on Rina who stood holding Sky, whose namesake tree had just been demolished. She reined in Wolfie by one finger hooked through a belt loop and spoke clearly in the unnatural quiet. "We certainly aren't the Waltons — are we?" Rina glanced around inquiringly at the immobilized troupe. "We were going to make our announcement later — but this suddenly seems like as good a time as any to tell you all something. Wolfie and I are moving to New Jersey. My company is transferring me and Wolfie won't have any trouble finding a job up there."

Wolfie and Rina both looked at Jane who still stood motionless. Without truly grasping the significance of her rebellious heart, Jane was in the process of deciding to do what *Jane* thought was best, not what was dictated by the family. She moved the corners of her mouth up into a smile and held her arms out in silent acceptance of Rina and Wolfie's decision.

Pandemonium erupted as Jane's mother began to sob anew. Rina handed the baby to Wolfie and put her face down very close to the old woman's and said softly, "Granny Mavis — Wolfie'll come back up here tomorrow and help you plant Sky another tree, and we'll come home for Christmas and hang some lights on it."

Mavis sniffed and mumbled something about her great grandson being raised as a Yankee and walked stiffly back to the house between Carol Lou and

Portia. Jane followed carrying Sky. She sat on the porch steps in easy conversation with her son and his wife as the day darkened into evening.

Rina and Wolfie left soon after the ice cream was served. Jane watched the fireworks that night through eyes that were finally beginning to see the light.

25

Mirror, Mirror

Ramona looked around the room full of women
with surreptitious curiosity. A women's bar . . . right
here in San Antonio. Well.

"What do you think?" Lu asked loudly above the
thumping bass of the dance music.

Before Ramona could answer, a dark shape
appeared at her right. She caught the amused glint in
Desiree's eyes as she looked up at a smallish young
man with punk-spikey blond hair, clad in black

leather from head to toe. Light glinted from high-heeled boots and a stunning array of chains and zippers.

"You b'long to someone?" The spikes jabbed a nod at the glass of beer Lu had ordered for the empty place in the booth to Ramona's left.

"Yeah — she belongs to us," Lu answered firmly. "We're a threesome."

Ramona felt a fiery blush color her upper body as the implication of Lu's words sunk in. She realized in another rush of embarrassment that the leather-boy was a leather-girl. As she walked away, the sway to those leather-covered hips was definitely female. Rawly, erotically, female. Ramona quickly drained the glass in front of her and reached for the one to her left.

"Whoa, there," Desiree cautioned, laying a perfectly manicured hand over her arm. "No need for anesthesia, honey. We'll protect you."

Ramona laughed at her own nervousness and relaxed a little as the beer did its work. Her knees still trembled from the sudden quiet that had moved through the crowd like a choreographed wave upon their entrance. Heads had turned, some politely, some plainly curious and quite a few in unabashed admiration of the three beautiful women moving into their arena.

"Howdy, folks."

Ramona glanced at Lu and Desiree before she allowed herself a peek up to see who now stood at the end of their table. A tall figure leaned in and across to receive an enthusiastic hug from Desiree and encircled the now standing Lu with long bony arms. Ramona sat expectantly, good-girl fashion, waiting to be introduced to the lanky woman who lifted Lu completely off her feet and swung her around in exuberant greeting.

"Put me down! Ya big *cowboy!*" Lu laughingly disentangled herself from the clutches of the woman who was obviously and old and much-loved friend.

"How long's it been, you two?" Big, capable, pinky-clean hands spread on the table as Ramona looked up into a freckled face wreathed with a changing, widening, easy smile. Engaging. Comfortable eyes. Crinkled in the corners with sincere pleasure at meeting old friends. And suddenly sparkling with something else as they settled on Ramona.

Ramona scooted over as Desiree shouted at the newcomer, "Sit down, LaRue. And put your eyeballs back in."

She turned to Ramona. "Ramona, meet an old friend of ours, Dixie LaRue. LaRue, this is Ramona Lee — a *new* friend of ours."

Doctor Dixie LaRue, M.D., bent her angular body into the right shape to fit the booth and sat. She took Ramona's hand firmly and raised it to her lips. "Charmed," she said in a honeyed baritone and, still holding Ramona's hand, turned to Desiree. "Okay, Parker. What's goin' on? You look different."

Desiree and Lu looked at each other and burst out laughing. "You're incredible, LaRue. Haven't seen you for two years and you pick up on our secret," Lu answered. "We're having a baby. But we're not pregnant yet!"

"Really? Hot damn. Are you gonna take a leave, Lu, or what?"

"Not me, pardner . . . Des."

LaRue released Ramona's hand and did a slack-jawed doubletake at Desiree. "You?"

"Yep."

"Well, lady — I . . . am . . . *impressed.*"

Ramona laced the fingers of both hands around her beer glass, determined not to be taken captive again as the other three women caught up on gossip. She finished off two more glasses of beer as the others laughed and reminisced. Then it was made clear to her in an uncomfortable rush that she was going to have to get up and walk across that room full of women — lesbian women — unless her bladder could be convinced to wait. It could not. Nope, definitely not!

She excused herself, moved rapidly past LaRue and made her way, with as much grace as she could muster, to the door marked SHE.

Waiting in line, she kept her eyes carefully busy with the machinations of a cuff button. She longed to get out of here and back home. Lu and Desiree had meant well. To show her some of the possibilities, they said. She would just have to get over this thing with Jane sooner or later. She must see that there were other women out there in the big world.

Ramona gratefully took her turn in the stall then made her way back across the small, temporarily quiet dance floor. The music began again. A slow and poignant fifties instrumental stabbed her chest and abdomen with a rush of longing and brought tears to her eyes. *Oh Jane — why? why?*

LaRue stood as if to allow her passage. Before Ramona knew what had happened, she was being guided across the floor by the pressure of LaRue's

160

strong, warm hand in the small of her back. Long legs against hers, hipbones fitting just slightly beneath her own, sliding past, meeting — moving — parting — slowly to the beat of the too-loud music.

"Relax, lady. We're dancing. Haven't you ever done this before?" LaRue's low breathy voice warmed Ramona's neck and ear. Something inside wasn't about to admit that this was the first time she'd danced with a woman. Something competitive from that place *oh-yeahs* lived in.

Ramona relaxed against the lightly insistent pressure of LaRue's arm across her shoulder and experienced the delicious shock of feeling another woman's breasts pressed against hers. The knowledge translated quickly to pleasurable pulsing between her legs. *Yes — ohgod yes. This is for me. I am a lesbian. Women excite me. Even strange women. But, I love Jane. I feel the wanting — but, it's Jane I want!*

Mercifully, the music ended as Ramona reached this emotional conclusion. She returned quickly to the booth, a few steps in front of LaRue, and caught Desiree's eye. "Please take me home," she whispered urgently, close to her friend's ear, and sat stiffly waiting as Desiree disengaged them from the moment.

Ramona made her face blank and pleasant as they said their goodbyes to LaRue, who looked regretfully puzzled. The warm night air washed over Ramona, caressing her with the heady scent of magnolias as she walked to the Jeep. The beer, the music, the wanting, settled into a knot in Ramona's stomach.

Four days since she had boldly kissed Jane goodbye . . . four days of a precious agony that threatened to go on forever. She suddenly needed a swim more than she needed air. The thought of

161

churning through the cool water possessed her thoughts as she gave Lu directions for the quickest route back home.

The three of them lost little time changing into swim clothes. Lu and Desiree donned T-shirts and cutoffs and joined Ramona, who was already swimming laps the length of the backyard pool. The sky was dark and starless as low scudding gulf clouds raced north overhead reflecting the city light, diffused and dancing, onto the swimmers.

Ten, twenty, twenty-five laps. Her arms and legs began to tire but she couldn't shake the ache in the pit of her stomach. Finally out of breath, she floated lazily, becoming slowly aware that Lu and Desiree were no longer in the pool. She stood in the shallow end, climbed out and sat heavily on a lounge beside the table where her two friends sat on a double swing embracing loosely — arms across shoulders, legs entwined — engrossed in each other. The soft sound of their laughter somehow freshened the ache she couldn't shake.

"Des, you and Lu help yourselves to whatever you need from the kitchen or wherever. I'm going to turn in now. I love you both . . . but I'm exhausted."

They rose and followed Ramona over the tiled path, through the atrium and into the cool house. "We're tired too, honey. We'll see you mañana." They headed for the guest room.

* * * * *

Ramona entered her bedroom and closed the door, peeling off her swimsuit as she moved toward the large bathroom. She stood nude in front of the white sink. Her skin reflected warmly in the large mirror. She felt strangely naked. She had stood here countless times before, but it had never felt like this. The full wall mirror behind her sent her reflection back at her — back and forth — hundreds of Ramona-bodies. Regimented breasts, dark pubic mounds, marched in unison, turned in formation.

She cupped her breasts in her hands. Her attention focused immediately on the sight of those woman-hands on her breasts. Images of Jane's hands filled her mind. LaRue's clean, pink hands on the table, then warm on her back. She moved her fingers lightly past her nipples. Her clitoris leaped as desire claimed her.

Ramona tentatively placed a hand on her stomach, slid her fingers downward, toward the suddenly flaming center of her being. Through the pleasantly furry hair, touching herself with a new awareness, hesitating only slightly before sliding a finger into the dark, soft-wet crevice. *Why have I never done this before?* Flashes of Jane exploded across her inner eye. Jane, eagerly astride her body — arching back — taut breasts straining toward the sky as orgasm gripped her.

An overpowering need for release insisted rhythmically on more strokes, faster. A very sane, very cool part of her mind examined her reflection in the mirror. High color on her cheeks, dark eyes flashing — mouth slightly open. She liked what she saw. And the liking embarrassed her.

Well, let's do this thing right, Ramona. Lying down would be nice. She smiled at her thoughts, then smiled more broadly yet at her mirror smile. She covered the space between the bathroom and her bed in three great strides and hurriedly climbed between the sheets. They settled cool over her bare body as she lost no time in resuming her quest for physical release. She loved herself in a new and uninhibited fashion.

Orgasm was not long in coming. She stiffened her legs and slowed her stroking fingers as breathtaking waves of pleasure racked her center — rolling, gathering, crashing — rolling out again.

More. She wanted more.

Her fingers began a light dance under the sheet, then faster as the urgency returned.

"Yikes! What the —"

Tiny spikes impaled her moving hand. Scrapper rolled and kicked at her captured prey with alarming tenacity for an old cat. Ramona grabbed Scrapper and rolled her onto her back, pummelling her playfully on the stomach. She scrabbled away from Ramona's grasp and strutted, bow-backed and hissing, along the edge of the bed, just out of reach.

"You old ratter! You're gonna lose your other ear if you don't watch out." She laughed and sucked at the finger where the cat had drawn blood. She grinned in spite of herself as the taste and smell of her recent passion sent a delicious thrill into her still lightly pulsing vagina.

Ramona pulled the covers back over her and lay thoughtfully still, listening to the spattering rain blow against the window. Scrapper padded close to her body, then lay purring against her neck. Ramona hugged the old cat and, much more quickly than she expected, slipped into sleep.

26

The Cello Speaks

The musicians assembled for the late summer exhibition performance. This was the "one for the money" after which the sponsors renewed their pledges. Or not. Depending on the quality of the performance, the food at the party, and/or whether or not the sponsor's personal fortune was in Texas oil or something more stable like Canadian real estate.

Jane wiped at the perspiration that continued to form at her temples and behind her ears. She wore a stiff white shirt and a full longish black skirt, belted in at the waist. Her feet were snuggled into soft black pierced-leather boots.

She was miserable.

She unfastened the metal closures of her cello case and opened the lid. The deep maroon wood was warm under her hand. The temperature inside the truck topper had probably reached 130 degrees before she'd made it out of the snarl of vehicles on Central Expressway. Expressway, hah! World's longest parking lot. She took the large, graceful instrument from its case and sat dreamily waiting for it to cool and contract to room temperature before she could touch the pegs for tuning.

The sensuous womanshape of the cello vividly recalled the memory of Ramona's beautiful torso, arching up toward her, their open vaginas touching, kissing a slow, grinding slippery kiss . . . Ramona's quick surprised gasp as orgasm gripped her. The memory of her delighted smile as she looked up at Jane from eyes sooty with sated desire.

Jane shook her head fiercely to clear the picture from her mind, but it was too late. Her body kept right on remembering and her breathing quickened as the conductor took the podium and raised her baton. This was it. The Borodin. Time to concentrate. The music would quell the memory.

She sat on the edge of the hard chair, her supple back piston straight. She spread her legs and firmly grasped the cello between her loosely skirted knees. Each stroke of the bow sent a heady thrumming through the wooden frame, centering tiny electric tremors in her warming vagina. She moved slightly against the chair as she swayed to the evocative

166

rhythm of the piece. She knew her performance had never been better, her cello never more passionate.

Each motion heightened her arousal. Faster and faster she moved, until, lost in the music, she came to sudden wrenching orgasm. Her knees jerked against the instrument, her booted feet rigid. Only the years of training enabled her to continue the piece. Habit took over when volition faltered.

Again and again she vibrated with the sound, until the piece was played through and she sat quietly spent, head bowed. Her loosened hair fell forward, her pulsing center sent out waves of exquisite pleasure.

The blood pounding in Jane's ears shut out the sounds of applause, then she flushed in sudden awareness of her abandon. The very boldness of her secret. So much for the music curing the ills of memory.

She knew now. She had to have Ramona or go mad. Whatever the cost.

There was no way to live the rest of her life without her. Not now, not after the explosion of passion they had ignited that night in the woods. Not now when even her music, a lifelong source of comfort, was no longer a safe haven.

* * * * *

The San Antonio city limits sign whizzed by Jane's window. God — what a whirl the last week since the concert had been. Back to work — catchup all week, then beg another week of vacation and go off to find out whether or not she had made the mistake of her life. It had been six whole weeks since the trek. Since . . . Ramona. Since Jane's life had turned inside out.

She touched her pocket for the hundredth time. The folded paper with Ramona's phone number on it was still there. She'd tried to make herself call from Dallas, but finally decided she would fare better if she was in the same city as Ramona when she called.

First Poppy had given her hell on the phone when she'd asked for Ramona's phone number. Then Kay was coolly reserved as she said maybe Jane'd better talk to Desiree before she called Ramona.

Every time she thought of Desiree's offhand remark that it might already be too late, her heart sank. What the blue hell did Desiree mean, a dance with a doctor had cured Ramona's heart condition?

After a frustrating full-circle snafu of missed or wrong exits, Jane finally navigated her way to Commerce Street and found parking. As she descended the bannistered stairway to the level of the river, her eyes, ears and nose took in the scintillating old-world *ambiente* of the Paseo del Rio — the River Walk. Bright colors banked and shimmered, reflected from the surface of the narrow, winding San Antonio River. Feathery palms guarded grand old balustraded hotels, and the sweet smell of magnolia filled the sparkling air. Bougainvillaea, banana trees and cannas flourished against the adobe walls and fountains along the flagstone walkway.

Jane walked for a while, then, weary and damp from the long hot drive, she sought the dark shade of a cypress and sat gratefully on a white wrought-iron bench. The sounds of lively mariachi music finally replaced the hum of the road in her inner ear. Pungent cooking smells wafted past on the light breeze. She watched two young lovers toss a coin into a gurgling fountain and ached with longing and apprehension.

Well Jane, this is it. Time to find a phone and find out. She walked, a little stiffly, shaking out the kinks, watching for the familiar sign of the Bell.

* * * * *

Brrruppp . . . brrrupp . . . Three, four five — six rings. Jane wiped her palms against her back pockets. Where was she? Why didn't she ans —.

"Hello."

Ramona! I love you. I can't live without you.

"Umm, hi . . . this is Jane . . . Jane Jackson. Remember me?"

Oh great. Where did that come from?

"Ooh. Yes, Jane." *Was that a chuckle?* "I remember you. How are you?"

"I'm here in San Antonio. I'd like to see you."

The tiny silence at the other end lengthened, measured in nanoseconds by Jane's pounding heart.

". . . Yes. We do need to see each other. But I'm sorry, I'm busy this evening. Will you be here long? Could we have lunch tomorrow? Where are you staying?"

Busy? Lunch? Staying?

"Umm . . . I . . . uh." Jane's frantic eye caught the name of the hotel lobby in which she was standing.

"La Mansion Del Rio." Thank God — whole articulate words were actually coming from her lips. "I'm staying at La Mansion. And I'd love to have lunch tomorrow."

169

"That's wonderful Jane — the restaurant there at the hotel is one of the best in the city. Is it okay if we meet there at one o'clock? It's good to hear your voice, Jane. I'm sorry I can't talk longer, but you've caught me just out of the shower. We'll catch up tomorrow. Okay? Oh — by the way — Saturday night on the Walk is exciting. Don't get carried away! See you tomorrow?"

"Yeah — tomorrow. OK Bye." *Just out of the shower — naked?*

"Bye."

Jane stood listening to the hum of the open line for a long moment while her heartbeat returned closer to normal. She hung up the phone slowly, cradling it with great care. A smile began and widened until it threatened to displace her ears. Then she remembered what Ramona had said.

Busy.

Busy doing what?

Well, at least she didn't hang up on me. That's something. But it's not enough — is it, Jungle Jane? Noooooo! Tomorrow — I will not think until tomorrow! Now, arrogant Janey. Now we will see if Providence has left us a vacancy in this marvelous hotel!

After a few sinking moments at the register desk while the clerk checked the computer for cancellations, Jane walked jauntily, room key in her pocket, back to move her truck to the hotel parking area.

Exciting. Yes — a good description of the evening revelries that she walked past and through. Young men and women from the nearby Air Force base enjoyed themselves as only the young really can.

170

Noisy oldsters dining aboard the barges pointed and snapped pictures as they glided past and disappeared under picturesque arched bridgeways.

Jane stopped at an inviting sidewalk cafe and ordered enchiladas. Her first meal since she had left Dallas early that morning.

Clicking castanets accompanied flamenco guitars as street dancers entertained a gathering crowd far below on another level. Jane watched one dancer in particular, a tall woman with her black hair piled high and secured by bright combs. Something about the way the woman moved recalled Ramona's moonlight dance to Ray's violin.

The tall dancer and her partner tapped their heels energetically to the rapid measures of the Spanish guitars. Jane turned forcibly away and centered her attention on the plate of aromatic enchiladas. Though she was hungry and the food delicious, her stomach sent messages that no more of the spicy meal would be tolerated. She tipped the handsome waiter and went off to re-park and get settled in the hotel room.

A steaming shower worked its magic and she was soon abed, between cool crisp sheets. She composed her thoughts, using her old mind control: *I will keep my mind off the things I don't want and on the things I do want.* Only . . . what she did want was Ramona. And thoughts of Ramona were not conducive to sleep.

She wandered to the window and back, paced, read and finally just lay on the bed, hoping sleep would simply sneak up on her.

It did — about four restless hours later.

27

Playing Fair

Morning was predictably disorienting. Jane had coffee and a bagel sent up, showered again and tipped a housekeeper to press the travel wrinkles from her best white cotton slacks and shirt.

Somehow — tick by tock, minute by slow, apprehension-filled minute — it was finally time to descend to the restaurant and wait for Ramona.

Jane chose a secluded corner table where she could watch Ramona's entrance. She had refolded and centered the napkins, rearranged the silverware to the correct centimeter of placement, checked her tanned and, she hoped, sophisticated image in the sides of the sweating water pitcher. She had just started to become seriously nervous when she sensed movement toward her table.

A canary-yellow swirl of ruffled flounces was choreographed into dance by Ramona's long easy stride as she approached Jane's corner. Her smile flashed white above a heart-stopping expanse of bared shoulders and shadowed collarbones. Inviting creamy breasts moved against an embroidered turquoise bodice.

"Jane!" Ramona held out both braceleted arms prompting the perfunctory woman-hug greeting. Large gold hops flashed at her ears. After a split second malfunction of her life-support system, Jane stood and saw in Ramona's dark eyes, to her unutterable delight, open appreciation of her appearance. Her blue eyes, her tan, the summery white pleated slacks and simple shirt were well received.

They hugged.

They sat.

They looked at each other.

The waiter appeared and they ordered lunch. A salad for Ramona and something with chicken and cheese for Jane.

Alone again, they both spoke at once.

"Why did you come?"

"Why did you meet me?"

"I wanted to see you again." This last simultaneously and laughed at. *Jinks. You owe me a lifetime.*

"But, why did —"

"What did —"

They grew shyly silent.

Jane held up a finger.

"My turn. You know, it's a good thing we're sitting down. Considering what happened a couple of time before when we were in similar situations."

Ramona's eyes were suddenly glassy with tears. Jane grasped her hand to comfort her and started guiltily as the waiter arrived with their meal.

Ramona pierced a cherry tomato with a plastic toothpick, again and again, like a child with no appetite, while Jane chased a bit of blue-corn tortilla with ice water.

Jane cleared her throat. Ramona's toothpick stopped its fencing maneuvers.

"Ramona, look at me."

Ramona complied. The beauty of her long curling lashes added to a surge of needy courage in Jane's heart.

"I love you, Pocahontas. I can't live without you."

Ramona sat silent for a heartbeat. "My God, Jane. Don't you know I feel the same way about you?" Her eyes brimmed with emotion and the raw beginnings of something else.

Jane's stomach lurched, her legs trembled and a wave of desire so strong it almost frightened her began to curl and gather power for its descent — its pulling energy peaked in her mind as a knowing confidence. A wild whitecap of delirious joy.

"Would you like to come upstairs with me now?" Jane's voice rasped with a low lusty nervousness. Her eyes never left Ramona's as she pulled bills from her pocket and placed them on the table. She then watched Ramona's body respond to her question as

174

Ramona's breath quickened and her breasts moved faster against the colorful fabric of her dress. She nodded and stood.

* * * * *

They were alone in the elevator. Jane barely managed to keep her arms from encircling those shoulders, her lips from seeking the lovely hollow of Ramona's throat. Ramona smiled at Jane. Suddenly they were in Jane's room with the door closed securely behind them.

Words — torrents of words — would come later but there was no need for them now. They kissed slowly, rediscovering each other. Holding, pressing closer. Jane's urgency grew intolerable. She steered Ramona toward the bed and pulled away in surprise as Ramona resisted.

"Let me."

There was no mistaking the meaning of Ramona's words as she began to unbutton Jane's shirt. The sight of her long, lacquered fingernails opening Jane's clothing sent Jane over the top of an imaginary hill. She trembled like a first-night ballerina in the wings — awaiting Ramona's next move.

Ramona completed Jane's disrobing with a slight hesitation now and again to step back and openly admire Jane's naked body. Jane made small moves toward Ramona but she was stopped by firm little shakes of Ramona's head.

Jane watched hungrily from her reclining position on the king-size bed as Ramona stood before her, turning fully — in open display of her own beautiful nakedness.

Then she moved languorously, closer — standing by the bed, towering above Jane now. Slowly she sat, then lifted her body over Jane's and lowered herself softly, deliciously onto the flushed, heated length of Jane's wanting, craving body. She kissed her mouth swiftly, then inched down to Jane's breasts and kissed her already hardened nipples. Not wetly. But dry — soft — with her lips. Jane pushed up to meet Ramona's mouth as it traveled downward still to nuzzle the soft mound of her stomach.

Jane's mind reeled, her senses exploded with the now certain knowledge of Ramona's intent. Her legs opened under Ramona's light pressure and she gasped at the luxurious feel of Ramona's heavy breasts sliding silky smooth over her thighs.

Ramona's warm breath bathed her groin, her upper thighs and centered purposefully over, then on, the cleft of her vulva. A shock of blue-hot desire pierced her body as Ramona's tongue, cool and tentative — then hot, insistent and probing, darted in, flicking across her clitoris. A few seconds — no more — and Jane arched up into the most explosive orgasm she'd ever experienced. She bounced wildly against Ramona's tongue, unable to stop the reaction of her starved psyche.

Ramona brought her lips quickly back up to Jane's mouth, moaning, wet, with the taste of Jane's passion covering her face. Her own need was urgent and evident now.

Jane's hand found Ramona's center. She moved it firmly against the direction of Ramona's thrusting hips. Ramona shuddered against her and settled limply by her side. Only then did she break their kiss.

"My God . . . Ramona. Where did you learn to do *that*?" Ramona grinned and lowered her lashes, hesitating only a moment before answering. "Oh, just something I picked up from a little green book."

Jane laughed and snuggled close to the woman she loved. Minutes turned into hours as they cuddled and caressed each other. They talked and laughed and cried. And finally they drifted into sleep, curled together like two half-grown cats.

* * * * *

Ramona woke first. She had never been so happy. Her mind was full with all the plans they had made. She would lease her house here in San Antonio and move to Dallas to live with Jane, while Jane satisfied the six-year obligation necessary to receive her retirement. Then they would travel.

Ramona rose on her elbow and watched Jane sleep. Slanting rays of evening sun peeked through where the drapes met. Fingers of hazy sunlight caressed Jane's lithe, strong body, forming inviting shadows across her buttocks and down into the small of her back. Desire rose in Ramona like a molten wave. Somehow ashamed of her urgency, she tried to quell the need, but her body, starved for so long, betrayed her. Her breathing quickened. She was achingly aware of exactly what she wanted.

Ramona laid her hand lightly on Jane's shoulder, letting her fingers caress Jane's silken skin. A throbbing need made itself known. She felt her pulse begin a rhythmic beat as blood rushed to her groin. She pulled her legs together and tensed her muscles, wiling her pulse to slow.

177

Jane stretched and turned toward Ramona. She smiled and very quickly responded to what Ramona thought must have been the look of utter desperation on her face.

"What's the matter, hon?" Jane teased. "Didn't you get enough loving?"

"Well . . . yes . . . no — I mean, I did, but I want you to . . . I want . . ." Ramona's voice trailed off as she agonizingly tried to put her need into words.

Jane sat up, her brows knitted in concern. "What is it, Ramona? Please . . . tell me."

"I want you to kiss me . . . down there." Ramona's voice lowered to an embarrassed whisper as she forced out the last words of her request.

"You do? Oh, thank God! . . . but I don't know how! I mean — I thought maybe I wasn't supposed to . . . or something — I mean — Oh God, this is all so new. I don't know the damned *rules*!"

Ramona pulled Jane's body onto hers. Then held her breath as Jane slid down until her cheek rested on Ramona's abdomen. Then she spread her legs apart for Jane's hesitant but amorous mouth, her steadily questing, then wildly probing tongue.

They made up the rules as they went along.

A few of the publications of
THE NAIAD PRESS, INC.
P.O. Box 10543 ● Tallahassee, Florida 32302
Phone (904) 539-5965
Mail orders welcome. Please include 15% postage.

VIRAGO by Karen Marie Christa Minns. 208 pp. Darsen has
chosen Ginny.   ISBN 0-941483-56-8 $8.95

WILDERNESS TREK by Dorothy Tell. 192 pp. Six women on
vacation learning "new" skills.   ISBN 0-941483-60-6   8.95

MURDER BY THE BOOK by Pat Welch. 256 pp. A Helen
Black Mystery. First in a series.   ISBN 0-941483-59-2   8.95

BERRIGAN by Vicki P. McConnell. 176 pp. Youthful Lesbian–
romantic, idealistic Berrigan.   ISBN 0-941483-55-X   8.95

LESBIANS IN GERMANY by Lillian Faderman & B. Eriksson.
128 pp. Fiction, poetry, essays.   ISBN 0-941483-62-2   8.95

THE BEVERLY MALIBU by Katherine V. Forrest. 288 pp. A
Kate Delafield Mystery. 3rd in a series. ISBN 0-941483-47-9   16.95

THERE'S SOMETHING I'VE BEEN MEANING TO TELL
YOU Ed. by Loralee MacPike. 288 pp. Gay men and lesbians
coming out to their children.   ISBN 0-941483-44-4   9.95
                                          ISBN 0-941483-54-1   16.95

LIFTING BELLY by Gertrude Stein. Ed. by Rebecca Mark. 104
pp. Erotic poetry.   ISBN 0-941483-51-7   8.95
                                          ISBN 0-941483-53-3   14.95

ROSE PENSKI by Roz Perry. 192 pp. Adult lovers in a long-term
relationship.   ISBN 0-941483-37-1   8.95

AFTER THE FIRE by Jane Rule. 256 pp. Warm, human novel
by this incomparable author.   ISBN 0-941483-45-2   8.95

SUE SLATE, PRIVATE EYE by Lee Lynch. 176 pp. The gay
folk of Peacock Alley are *all* cats.   ISBN 0-941483-52-5   8.95

CHRIS by Randy Salem. 224 pp. Golden oldie. Handsome Chris
and her adventures.   ISBN 0-941483-42-8   8.95

THREE WOMEN by March Hastings. 232 pp. Golden oldie. A
triangle among wealthy sophisticates.   ISBN 0-941483-43-6   8.95

RICE AND BEANS by Valeria Taylor. 232 pp. Love and
romance on poverty row.   ISBN 0-941483-41-X   8.95

PLEASURES by Robbi Sommers. 204 pp. Unprecedented
eroticism.   ISBN 0-941483-49-5   8.95

EDGEWISE by Camarin Grae. 372 pp. Spellbinding
adventure.   ISBN 0-941483-19-3   9.95

FATAL REUNION by Claire McNab. 216 pp. 2nd Det. Inspec.
Carol Ashton mystery.   ISBN 0-941483-40-1   8.95

WE WALK THE BACK OF THE TIGER by Patricia A. Murphy. 192 pp. Romantic Lesbian novel/beginning women's movement.
ISBN 0-941483-13-4   8.95

SUNDAY'S CHILD by Joyce Bright. 216 pp. Lesbian athletics, at last the novel about sports.   ISBN 0-941483-12-6   8.95

OSTEN'S BAY by Zenobia N. Vole. 204 pp. Sizzling adventure romance set on Bonaire.   ISBN 0-941483-15-0   8.95

LESSONS IN MURDER by Claire McNab. 216 pp. 1st Det. Inspec. Carol Ashton mystery — erotic tension!.   ISBN 0-941483-14-2   8.95

YELLOWTHROAT by Penny Hayes. 240 pp. Margarita, bandit, kidnaps Julia.   ISBN 0-941483-10-X   8.95

SAPPHISTRY: THE BOOK OF LESBIAN SEXUALITY by Pat Califia. 3d edition, revised. 208 pp.   ISBN 0-941483-24-X   8.95

CHERISHED LOVE by Evelyn Kennedy. 192 pp. Erotic Lesbian love story.   ISBN 0-941483-08-8   8.95

LAST SEPTEMBER by Helen R. Hull. 208 pp. Six stories & a glorious novella.   ISBN 0-941483-09-6   8.95

THE SECRET IN THE BIRD by Camarin Grae. 312 pp. Striking, psychological suspense novel.   ISBN 0-941483-05-3   8.95

TO THE LIGHTNING by Catherine Ennis. 208 pp. Romantic Lesbian 'Robinson Crusoe' adventure.   ISBN 0-941483-06-1   8.95

THE OTHER SIDE OF VENUS by Shirley Verel. 224 pp. Luminous, romantic love story.   ISBN 0-941483-07-X   8.95

DREAMS AND SWORDS by Katherine V. Forrest. 192 pp. Romantic, erotic, imaginative stories.   ISBN 0-941483-03-7   8.95

MEMORY BOARD by Jane Rule. 336 pp. Memorable novel about an aging Lesbian couple.   ISBN 0-941483-02-9   9.95

THE ALWAYS ANONYMOUS BEAST by Lauren Wright Douglas. 224 pp. A Caitlin Reese mystery. First in a series.
ISBN 0-941483-04-5   8.95

SEARCHING FOR SPRING by Patricia A. Murphy. 224 pp. Novel about the recovery of love.   ISBN 0-941483-00-2   8.95

DUSTY'S QUEEN OF HEARTS DINER by Lee Lynch. 240 pp. Romantic blue-collar novel.   ISBN 0-941483-01-0   8.95

PARENTS MATTER by Ann Muller. 240 pp. Parents' relationships with Lesbian daughters and gay sons.
ISBN 0-930044-91-6   9.95

THE PEARLS by Shelley Smith. 176 pp. Passion and fun in the Caribbean sun.   ISBN 0-930044-93-2   7.95

MAGDALENA by Sarah Aldridge. 352 pp. Epic Lesbian novel set on three continents.   ISBN 0-930044-99-1   8.95

THE BLACK AND WHITE OF IT by Ann Allen Shockley.
144 pp. Short stories.   ISBN 0-930044-96-7   7.95

SAY JESUS AND COME TO ME by Ann Allen Shockley. 288
pp. Contemporary romance.   ISBN 0-930044-98-3   8.95

LOVING HER by Ann Allen Shockley. 192 pp. Romantic love
story.   ISBN 0-930044-97-5   7.95

MURDER AT THE NIGHTWOOD BAR by Katherine V.
Forrest. 240 pp. A Kate Delafield mystery. Second in a series.
                                      ISBN 0-930044-92-4   8.95

ZOE'S BOOK by Gail Pass. 224 pp. Passionate, obsessive love
story.   ISBN 0-930044-95-9   7.95

WINGED DANCER by Camarin Grae. 228 pp. Erotic Lesbian
adventure story.   ISBN 0-930044-88-6   8.95

PAZ by Camarin Grae. 336 pp. Romantic Lesbian adventurer
with the power to change the world. ISBN 0-930044-89-4   8.95

SOUL SNATCHER by Camarin Grae. 224 pp. A puzzle, an
adventure, a mystery — Lesbian romance.   ISBN 0-930044-90-8   8.95

THE LOVE OF GOOD WOMEN by Isabel Miller. 224 pp.
Long-awaited new novel by the author of the beloved *Patience
and Sarah*.   ISBN 0-930044-81-9   8.95

THE HOUSE AT PELHAM FALLS by Brenda Weathers. 240
pp. Suspenseful Lesbian ghost story. ISBN 0-930044-79-7   7.95

HOME IN YOUR HANDS by Lee Lynch. 240 pp. More stories
from the author of *Old Dyke Tales*. ISBN 0-930044-80-0   7.95

EACH HAND A MAP by Anita Skeen. 112 pp. Real-life poems
that touch us all.   ISBN 0-930044-82-7   6.95

SURPLUS by Sylvia Stevenson. 342 pp. A classic early Lesbian
novel.   ISBN 0-930044-78-9   7.95

PEMBROKE PARK by Michelle Martin. 256 pp. Derring-do
and daring romance in Regency England.   ISBN 0-930044-77-0   7.95

THE LONG TRAIL by Penny Hayes. 248 pp. Vivid adventures
of two women in love in the old west. ISBN 0-930044-76-2   8.95

HORIZON OF THE HEART by Shelley Smith. 192 pp. Hot
romance in summertime New England.   ISBN 0-930044-75-4   7.95

AN EMERGENCE OF GREEN by Katherine V. Forrest. 288
pp. Powerful novel of sexual discovery.   ISBN 0-930044-69-X   8.95

THE LESBIAN PERIODICALS INDEX edited by Claire
Potter. 432 pp. Author & subject index.   ISBN 0-930044-74-6   29.95

DESERT OF THE HEART by Jane Rule. 224 pp. A classic;
basis for the movie *Desert Hearts*. ISBN 0-930044-73-8   7.95

SPRING FORWARD/FALL BACK by Sheila Ortiz Taylor.
288 pp. Literary novel of timeless love.   ISBN 0-930044-70-3 7.95

CURIOUS WINE by Katherine V. Forrest. 176 pp. Passionate
Lesbian love story, a best-seller. ISBN 0-930044-43-6 8.95

BLACK LESBIAN IN WHITE AMERICA by Anita Cornwell.
141 pp. Stories, essays, autobiography. ISBN 0-930044-41-X 7.50

CONTRACT WITH THE WORLD by Jane Rule. 340 pp.
Powerful, panoramic novel of gay life. ISBN 0-930044-28-2 9.95

MRS. PORTER'S LETTER by Vicki P. McConnell. 224 pp.
The first Nyla Wade mystery. ISBN 0-930044-29-0 7.95

TO THE CLEVELAND STATION by Carol Anne Douglas.
192 pp. Interracial Lesbian love story. ISBN 0-930044-27-4 6.95

THE NESTING PLACE by Sarah Aldridge. 224 pp. A
three-woman triangle—love conquers all! ISBN 0-930044-26-6 7.95

THIS IS NOT FOR YOU by Jane Rule. 284 pp. A letter to a
beloved is also an intricate novel. ISBN 0-930044-25-8 8.95

FAULTLINE by Sheila Ortiz Taylor. 140 pp. Warm, funny,
literate story of a startling family. ISBN 0-930044-24-X 6.95

THE LESBIAN IN LITERATURE by Barbara Grier. 3d ed.
Foreword by Maida Tilchen. 240 pp. Comprehensive bibliography.
Literary ratings; rare photos. ISBN 0-930044-23-1 7.95

ANNA'S COUNTRY by Elizabeth Lang. 208 pp. A woman
finds her Lesbian identity. ISBN 0-930044-19-3 6.95

PRISM by Valerie Taylor. 158 pp. A love affair between two
women in their sixties. ISBN 0-930044-18-5 6.95

BLACK LESBIANS: AN ANNOTATED BIBLIOGRAPHY
compiled by J. R. Roberts. Foreword by Barbara Smith. 112 pp.
Award-winning bibliography. ISBN 0-930044-21-5 5.95

THE MARQUISE AND THE NOVICE by Victoria Ramstetter.
108 pp. A Lesbian Gothic novel. ISBN 0-930044-16-9 6.95

OUTLANDER by Jane Rule. 207 pp. Short stories and essays
by one of our finest writers. ISBN 0-930044-17-7 8.95

ALL TRUE LOVERS by Sarah Aldridge. 292 pp. Romantic
novel set in the 1930s and 1940s. ISBN 0-930044-10-X 7.95

A WOMAN APPEARED TO ME by Renee Vivien. 65 pp. A
classic; translated by Jeannette H. Foster. ISBN 0-930044-06-1 5.00

These are just a few of the many Naiad Press titles — we are the oldest and largest lesbian/feminist publishing company in the world. Please request a complete catalog. We offer personal service; we encourage and welcome direct mail orders from individuals who have limited access to bookstores carrying our publications.